HAVE
YOU
SEEN

ME?

ELIZABETH

GRAVER

THE ECCO PRESS

Published in 1993 by The Ecco Press
100 West Broad Street, Hopewell, NJ 08525
First published in hardcover by the University of Pittsburgh Press in 1991

This edition by arrangement with the University of Pittsburgh Press

Library of Congress Cataloging-in-Publication Data

Graver, Elizabeth, 1964–
      Have you seen me? / Elizabeth Graver.
         p.   cm.
      Contents: Around the world—Have you seen me?—Yellow tent—The blue
   hour—Scraps—The boy who fell forty feet—The experimental forest—The
   body shop—Music for four doors—The counting game.
      : $9.95
      I. Title.
   [PS3557.R2864H38   1993]   813. '.54—dc20   92-13372   CIP
      ISBN 0-88001-286-2

A CIP catalogue record for this book is available from the British Library.

The following stories, some in slightly different form, first appeared in the follow-
ing publications: *Antæus* ("Have You Seen Me?"); *Prism International* ("The Blue
Hour"); *Seventeen* ("The Counting Game"); *The Southern Review* ("The Body
Shop"); *Southwest Review* ("Yellow Tent"); *The Stanford Humanities Review*
("The Boy Who Fell Forty Feet"); and *Story* ("Around the World," published as
"Square Dance").
      Grateful acknowledgment is made for permission to reprint lyrics from "San
Francisco" by Maxime Le Forestier, © 1973 by Editions Coincidences, 31, rue
Francois 1 er, 75 008 Paris. Lines from "Infant Innocence" by A. E. Housman are
adapted with permission of Charles Scribner's Sons, an imprint of Macmillan
Publishing Company, from *My Brother, A. E. Housman*, by Laurence Housman;
copyright 1937, 1938 by Laurence Housman; renewal copyright © 1965, 1966 by
Lloyds Bank Ltd. Permission also granted by the Society of Authors as the literary
representative of the Estate of A. E. Housman and Jonathan Cape Ltd., publishers
of A. E. Housman's *Collected Poems*.
      These stories are as much a part of my community as they are of my own
private effort. For their combination of boundless faith and keen-eyed criticism, I
would like to thank my Cambridge writers' group—Audrey Schulman, Lauren
Slater and Pagan Kennedy—as well as Roy Kasten, Susan Bernofsky, Juda Bennett,
Ralph Savarese, my parents, Lawrence and Suzanne Graver, and my sister, Ruth
Graver. Thanks, as well, to the students and teachers in the writing programs at
Washington University in St. Louis and Cornell University, especially Stanley
Elkin, for his close attention to this collection. I am grateful to the Spencer T. Olin
Foundation for providing financial support during the writing of these stories, and
to my agent, Richard Parks, for his mixture of gentleness and persistence in
helping them find homes.

For my mother and father

CONTENTS

HAVE
YOU
SEEN
ME?

AROUND THE WORLD

The radio says bad cold spell, so I go about the house and dress myself for warmth and company. First my own long underwear top, whose pink weave fits me like a skin. Then the brace, Kyra's flannel shirt, my mother's sweater, Kyra's woolen tights, and on top of those, Robin's baggy jeans held up with a purple sash. Most of the clothes I put on have been left out, draped over chairs or tossed in the corner of someone's room. A few I rummage for in closets, knowing they'll be there. Finally, I wrap a scarf around my neck, zip myself into my father's blue down jacket, and go out to the creaking front porch to sit for a few minutes before work. At first, as I ease myself onto the porch steps, I smell only the wood stacked there, the bunched frozen air, but then as I bring my knees up to my chest the smells of my layers come to me, my family on my back.

"Stay in, Hannah," I imagine my father saying, but I welcome the cold air seeping through the boards to my behind and remember a fever I had when I was twelve, how my parents sat me down in a cold tub and sang me off-key rounds until my fever broke.

I could, if I needed to, stay in this house forever. This is what I tell myself, that they would never kick me out; they have plenty of room and adequate money, big hearts. They love me, yes, because I am theirs and came out with the right number of toes and fingers and a head of amazing orange hair. And grew up the oldest and tallest, the best cook, fastest runner, and only fiddle player, and then in eleventh grade gym Ian Nisbet asked me to square dance, and we do-si-doed and joined hands and went around the world, and in half a second he had ripped something so hard from my neck down to my elbow that the whole gym twitched like ganglia, and I felt it in my eyes, my back, liquid for an instant, searing, and then the pain hardened, settled, and became solid and determined, lodged like chiggers beneath my skin.

4

Since then I have shifted my expectations, or rather every time I try to read a thread of pain runs from my eyes down to my back, and each time I lift my left hand my wrist tightens like hot, braided wire, and my fingers splay. I am, if nothing else, the mystery of East Coast neurologists, with my untraceable dislodged nerve. Angry? How can you blame someone for dancing you too hard, though I never liked him, and when I hear he has graduated from college now and lived in Seattle, San Francisco, New York, I wonder what it was about that spin that sent him whirling in his Southern Comfort T-shirt and left me crouching on the varnished floor.

And around now my family must be slinging their shoes over their shoulders and walking barefoot toward an empty patch of beach, and my nearsighted father is counting heads and reciting landmarks: "Remember, guys, we're right near the red umbrella. Look for the stripes when you get out." Go on, kiddo, be brave; show them your swimsuit, I think to Robin, who is more confident in cold weather, where he comes off vaguely cute and padded, like a bear. Kyra has crocheted herself a bikini, tiny and ready to unravel on her happy flesh. She must be belly down on her towel now, glistening with coconut oil, the best vacationer. "Do you want a T-shirt or a tacky plastic something?" she asked before they left.

And now the dog is bounding toward me with a dead rabbit in his mouth, so I say, "Ugh, Utah, get away, you foul thing," and he shakes his head and wheels around, back into the brush. I would like to stay and listen to him plow through the dry sticks, but I have to take my vitamins and pills before Jacob, the new custodian, comes over to drive me to work.

"Utah!" I shout, my voice shrill in the wide yard. "Utah!"

Then he is back, stretching toward me across the snow, his jaws empty this time, eyes on me. "Come here," I say. "Let's go in." He comes to where I sit on the porch steps, puts his head against my knees, and slowly I lower my cheek to his bony forehead and hold him against me until he shakes himself free.

5

"Yes, I'm going to feed you," I tell him. "Yes. Then you're on your own because I've got to go."

Once, I had no patience with people who talked to animals. I disliked teenagers who stayed home for the summer, kids who didn't go to college, especially the smart ones who failed their high school courses because they'd rather get stoned and drive around in souped-up cars. I looked down on many things: prefabricated houses, lawn ornaments, loud makeup, bad grammar, the inability to get off your ass and look for anything better than what you had. The fall I should have gone to college I was too tired all the time, too weary from the aching of my eyes. At home I napped in my room, woke and memorized anatomy books. When my eyes and nerves drove me from the page, I quizzed my sister on her times tables, bit my nails until the sides were pink like raw meat, got my mother to take me on long car rides into Vermont, and scowled at the bright, unfolding mountains, all that fall.

Still, there were friends I saw now and then, people left over from high school, the un-college-bound: a girl named Kelly who lived on a farm near the mountain and raised goats; Paula Canadish, who got pregnant in ninth grade and dropped out of school to have her baby; Darrell, with his long New England face and stubborn chin, who did electrical work and kissed me one morning in our basement, which he was rewiring. Slow and careful, that kiss, his arms held flat against his sides, and he drew back in the middle and said to tell him if it hurt. I found myself digging my fingernails into my palms, almost crying, and I said, "For Christ's sake, how could it hurt—it's only my goddamn mouth!"

6

Then we kissed once more against the damp concrete, and as he started to undo things, my shirt, my brace, I remembered times before the dance with other guys, how much I had needed to feel skin against me, anything.

"No," I said, because I couldn't go back to that.

And he told me he'd been watching me for years. My track meets, my hair, everything.

"Leave me alone," I told him, "or I'll call the police."

"Shit," he said, in a quiet voice. "You probably really would."

I laughed then and said it was a joke, that I was sorry, but I was not sorry, and then winter came, and spring, and that summer I was more tired than I'd ever been, sleeping all day under a sheet with the fan going high speed, or on a foam mat in the side yard with the pain prodding me like a stick. Mostly it was my left arm that gave me trouble, and my eyes. Sometimes I felt small explosions like bubbles popping in my back and feet; when I tried to bend, my neck and back brace held my torso upright as a porcelain doll's. And there were my younger brothers and sisters growing taller every day: Kyra so pretty you wanted to stop things before they turned sour; Jessie a ringleader, followed about by the neighbors' three little kids; Robin building his model boats in the cool basement, and once, when I caught him by surprise, he was just in his underwear down there, hunched over the skeleton of his wooden ship.

By the end of the summer, the world seemed wrapped in sleep, and something had moved through me like a sigh. My parents had connections in town, people anxious to help out (such a pretty girl, such a bright girl, such a shame). When I was offered a job as a part-time monitor in the children's room of the library, I took it graciously and performed it cheerfully, and later, when I started getting headaches from the fluorescent lights, I was offered a job working at the local college taking care of the tiny zoological museum and told them yes.

"If we approach it right," said the neurologists, "limited exercise of this sort could be just the thing," and most of the time it was all right, although I never knew when the pain would sneak up from behind. It has turned into four years, feeding the scorpions, dusting the stuffed kangaroo, organizing exhibits on the sounds of dolphins and habitats of bats. Have I compromised myself? My parents tell me not to worry, I'm still young.

"Get your health back," they say, "then we'll see."

The museum is one big room attached to the biology building—panes of glass and tanks of animals, waxed wooden floors and my desk in the corner next to a stuffed moose mottled from the hands of students and the wear of time.

I am ready for work at nine, but Jacob pulls up ten minutes late—the snow, he says, combing his hair with his fingers, but I am skeptical and think of Mr. Carol, the steady old custodian who used to call me Mrs. Zoo and accepted the extra duty of picking me up with good grace. Slouched over the wheel in his green pickup truck, Jacob mutters something about how wiped out he is. "Played late last night," he says, and I make a noncommittal, conversational grunt.

When I get to work I unlock the doors and hang the monkey-shaped Open sign on its hook. The museum is small but visited frequently by college students and kids from the public schools, and people in town look out for the collection. Many of the dead animals are locals: the owl crashed into a Greek professor's window and was brought in to be stuffed; the groundhog was found frozen but intact in a mound of snow. The other animals, the live ones, come from farther off, and I have repainted the backdrops of their cages to mimic tundra, jungle, desert, forest floor. In the far corner is the bones section and the glass cupboard full of jars—a heart in formaldehyde, a floating frog, a tiny human fetus, white and curled as a hand in pain.

And because it is their school vacation, the children stop by to see the sights or warm up between sledding trips on the steep hill behind the quad. Some of them know me, some don't, but I do not intimidate, though the top of my brace pokes out of my sweater like an extra limb. I feed the animals from the narrow hallway around back, which runs the length of the tanks. Peering through, I can also survey my tiny kingdom from behind the scenes. The menu does not vary much from day to day, although in summer I bring in garden vegetables as treats. Most days I put the same quantity of food in the same corner of each cage, and they nose over, open their pink or black, sharp or toothless mouths, take what is offered, and go on.

The only exception, the only bit of razzmatazz, is the boa, christened Trance because when she arrived at the museum she lay for days in a tight coil, her long head swaying slightly as if following a slow, invisible pendulum back and forth. Each morning the head of biology deposited a mouse in the snake's cage and hovered over her, and each morning, as the mouse hugged corners and ran circles, Trance simply sat. Until the tenth day, when a particularly sensitive mouse's legs gave out, and the snake flicked her tongue, unwound, killed the animal with a professional squeeze, and swallowed it, settling on the floor of her cage to digest.

She was the only live animal in the museum who all the visitors swore was stuffed. Children could bang on her glass cage with their dirty fists, ignoring the Don't Touch signs, and she would lie still as the clay coil pots they made in school. The professors could flash lights in her eyes, adjust the levels on her heat lamp, play the radio at top volume above her cage, and Trance wouldn't twitch. Except when she saw the mouse, and then some muscle-moving, blood-quickening reaction tripped down her thick trunk, and the snake's dull body eased into motion, uncurling on its

8

branch—sliding, sometimes, down the backdrop of fronds and sky, and she squeezed for her supper, and swallowed whole, and returned to her sluggish state.

I am choosing the mouse of the day when the Brownies come in. The mice are kept in the back corridor with the other food, their cages dank and cramped. I pick a mouse with about as much interest as I pick one blueberry from a bowlful; this has been going on a long time. The one I choose is as small, white, and quick as the others, and I scoop it into a coffee can with a one-handed motion and turn to give Trance her fix.

But there on the other side, flat against the glass, are six beating hands belonging to three small Brownies doing their best to pound Trance from her dreams. From my angle up above, I can see only the girls' palms and their brown berets, but I hear their shrill voices: "Ooooh, lookit; I told you he was big. How come he doesn't move? How come it's just lying there? I bet he's dead, huh? Yoohoo Mr. Snakey! Hey!"

I could go out, I think, and scold them for touching, then give them my standard talk about the snake. They are younger than Jessie, around eight, probably. They must have just gotten out of their meeting, cutting across campus to go home. I am tipping the coffee can in my hand, and then the mouse is skidding up the side, trying to bite my fingers with its frantic teeth, and I whisper, "Shit, you little bastard," and fling it in.

Which is when one of the Brownies screams so loud that every creature in every cage seems to stop for a moment to listen.

"Ahhh!" she shrieks. "He's gonna kill it, he's gonna kill it!"

And, indeed, Trance lifts her head, swings round her thick body, and begins to curve toward the mouse.

"No!" hollers the girl, and by this time I have left my hallway and am there to grab her from behind as she throws herself at the glass front of the cage.

In spirit I am there to pull her back, in intention, but as I

9

tell my arm to reach for her, the tensing up begins within my veins, the freezing up like pistons without oil. The tunneling in, so that when it happens, my body becomes the entire feeling world, and although I can see the girl's face, the room, the animals, the glare of snow outside, essentially they are not there. In the beginning, the first few times, I thought it would last forever, this narrowing—my fingers curling toward my palms, my tongue toward my throat, my abdomen and stomach pulled back, reaching like a heated magnet for my spine. Gradually, it always went away. Like a developing photograph, the room would gain color and ease into focus. My body would lose its grip on itself, and there I'd be, and there would be the world in its prior state, impassive and clear.

"Listen to me," I say calmly to the girl, though my arms hang limp at my sides. "Please stop. You'll scare her."

But she is beating her hands against the glass, pounding her head as her friends look on.

"I told you to get away from that cage," I say. "You're going to break the glass."

The child flails an arm in my direction as if to push me away, but when I step back, she changes tactics, turning now to me.

"Get him out! Get the mouse! Please get him out!"

She throws herself against me, tugs on my sweater, and I turn my good side toward her, put my hand over her eyes and hold her there, thinking of Robin and Jessie the time our father caught his hand in the garage door and lost half a finger, how the two of them hid behind the stacked lawn furniture, ducking their heads into their arms; how terribly calm I'd been. When I uncover the girl's eyes and let her go, she is still sobbing, her mouth slack. She puts one arm around me for a second as if I am a logical comforter, then pulls back with a whining noise.

"Shhh," I say to her, the room, myself. "Okay? Calm down."

On the beach, my family must be eating lunch, sandy hot

dogs and chips, and my father is making sure everyone gets a fair share, and Robin is saying he is not hungry and throwing flirtatious sidelong glances at the food. We eat chicken, I want to tell the girl. We eat hot dogs. If this mouse did not die here, it would be injected with some chemical, or fastened to wires, or given ungodly amounts of artificial sweeteners, and even if it ran free in a big, wheat-filled, mice-filled field, even then, one day, this mouse would die, perhaps in the jaws of a snake.

11

But the girl has turned toward the fish tank, her arms wrapped around her middle, her cotton Brownie uniform hiked up at the waist. She brushes at her nose with the back of her hand.

"Is she okay?" I ask her friends, who refuse to look at me. "She has to eat," I inform the room. "Snakes eat mice. It's Nature."

Under the high ceiling, my voice sounds like a loud recording, but not even the animals look up. The girl sniffles and then, as we all stand watching, a dark stream appears on her wrinkled brown tights and forms a puddle on the floor. She turns and looks down, then over at me, and something like a willed half-smile appears on her face—forgiveness or revenge. She leans over, steps out of her rubber boots, takes off her tights and underpants, and puts her boots back on. Then she turns to go, leaving the soiled garments on the floor.

"You need those. It's freezing cold outside," I call. "Hang on!"

But she has grabbed her red parka from the corner, put on her mittens, and the others are following behind, out to the cold blast which I feel as if it were circling my legs. It will burn her bare skin, but there is nothing I can do. Although Trance is busy digesting, there are still the scorpions to deal with, the tarantula and hamsters, the ailing bat.

Once, I think, as I maneuver her wet tights and underwear into a plastic bag, once I was a Brownie in this town and won badges for building fires and weaving baskets, for jumping on the trampoline and helping at the nursing home, where I did cartwheels for the men between their beds. What I want to tell the girl, what the realist in me wants to say is: toughen up. Trance has her problems, and so do all white mice, and so do you and I. It is what I would say, if she were to come back, but she is gone. Probably she is home now, getting new panties, changing into her snow pants, and then they will go sledding on the hill, stretching their necks, screaming and tumbling like badgers in the snow.

More than anything, I want to cry. Not because it is so sad—God knows, there are worse things than a dead white mouse or the spirited anger of a Brownie. But at first I couldn't do it either. I would feed the other animals their grains, pellets, and bits of green, then Mr. Carol would come on his cleaning rounds and I'd say, "Hey, I hate to ask again, Mr. Carol," and while I sat at my desk pretending not to watch, he would go around back, grab a mouse by the tail, and drop it in.

"All set, Mrs. Zoo," he would say, pulling his cart of cleaning supplies past my desk. "Everybody's got to eat."

And those were the days when I memorized books, trooped off to doctor after doctor, took test after test, and when that didn't work, read up on acupuncture and herbal healing. And touched myself at night, alone in bed, experimenting with what hurt too much, circling my good hand up and down like the most expert lover.

In front of my family, I cried. All the time, so often that they learned to keep the conversation going when the streams began, as if it had simply started raining or someone had turned on the faucet at the kitchen sink. There I was, so tired after a while, wiped out, and then Mr. Carol died of a stroke, leaving me little choice because the new custodian was young and sullen and told me he planned to become famous in a rock band, and I was nothing if not proud.

On the way home from work, I mention the girl, and

Jacob says, "Jesus Christ, only a kid from this town could get so riled up about a goddamn mouse."

"What do you mean?" I ask, and he turns halfway toward me and makes a whistling noise through his teeth.

"Fucking Never-Never Land," he says. "Doesn't she have anything better to think about?"

"She's a kid. Everything is relative, I guess."

But Jacob is busy complaining about his green janitor's uniform, and the way a chemistry professor spoke to him today, and how nobody cares about anything in this stupid town, in this stupid country for that matter.

"You get your little house," he says, "and you get your little wife, tra la la, and then you go zooming around in your car and isn't life the greatest?"

"Aw, shit," he says then, and stops abruptly at a stop sign so that we jerk forward and my hand flies to my neck. I suck in my breath.

"For God's sake," I say. "Could you drive a little more carefully?"

He stops talking and slows down drastically so that the car behind us honks and tries to pass.

"Go ahead," says Jacob, glancing in the rearview mirror. "Pass me, old fellow. Go wild!"

He swerves the truck over onto the shoulder, and the station wagon moves ahead.

"Hold on tight," he says, pulling slowly back into the road. "We're off!"

Then we are at my driveway, in front of my door, and I get out without a good-bye, thinking it serves him right, almost forgetting my yellow knapsack, but he picks it up from the seat and hands it to me.

"If you're planning to be late again tomorrow," I say, "please call."

"Planning to be late," he says. "Ha."

Then the departure: slamming door, spinning tires on the icy drive, three short honks, and he has grazed a snowbank and skidded back onto the road. When he rounds the corner, nothing is left but the aftermath of the honk in my ears and Utah sending staccato sounds out over the front porch, barking as if there were something to protect.

Inside, I play a record, put on water for tea, and run a bath. Usually, around now, I am helping with dinner, but with them gone, I wander the house in my stocking feet, trailing my hand on countertops and walls. When I was little, accumulation seemed the norm to me, but now, as I catalogue, I am amazed—how they managed it, not only buying the shell of the house, but filling it with furniture and children and kitchen drawers full of years' worth of recipes, bread ties, rubber bands. All this from two people who were not even related once, who met at a walkathon for charity, both of them well-intentioned but cursed with blisters, lagging behind. My family does not take pictures; just as well—we are an odd-looking bunch, disparate in size, shape, and color. But in the bathroom is a framed family portrait I drew when I was twelve. We are standing in a line—Robin thinner than life, Kyra plainer, Utah's mother Limerick and I blazing with red hair. I hold my lacrosse stick like a scepter.

I cannot say I haven't learned some things since then. Because of its slow metabolism, the red legs tarantula can survive in the desert without food for over two and a half years, waiting for insects and lizards to wander within reach. Other creatures are more aggressive: a locust will eat its own weight in a day. Half the game involves hiding, the other half knowing how to ruffle the plumage or flash the orange dot. Slowly, I undress before the family portrait. From its place on the wall, it has seen a long parade of bathers over the years, a baring of our various private selves. I grip the steel bar alongside the tub and lower myself through the steam. My limp white limbs are perfect underwater, there where every edge is muted, movement slowed.

At work the next day I pick-type an index card, arrange a file, wipe down a pane of glass. We have arrived early; I am prey to Jacob's schedule, and he had to move equipment into a chemistry lab before the first class. At feeding time I move down the back corridor. I am halfway through when I hear the approaching roar of the vacuum cleaner and look through the hamster tank to see Jacob pushing his way across the floor.

And I am not sure why I do it, because it's not as if I can't deal with these things myself, but I wipe my hand on my jeans and go out.

I yell. "Hey, could you do me a favor?"

"Huh?" he shouts back.

"A *favor!* Can you help me with something? "

Jacob turns off the machine. In the abrupt silence, I remember Mr. Carol—his slow, wide face, his head too big for his body, the neat haircut, the sideburns trimmed in a gray line. His uniform was always ironed, his name embroidered in red script above the breast pocket. Jacob wears his uniform rumpled and unclean, the way teenagers wear army surplus, as a look.

"Sorry," I say. "I mean, I know you're working, but I was wondering—after yesterday, this mouse thing is just bugging me. If the kid comes back or something, and I'm in the middle of feeding Trance . . . "

He squints, tucks his chin toward his neck. I look away.

"What the hell is Trance?"

I turn to her cage. Jacob swivels to see her immobile on her branch.

"She hardly ever eats," I tell him. "One a day for two days, then two weeks with nothing. I just—"

"Look," he says, "the kid's not gonna come back. Not two days in a row, so then you've got two weeks for her to forget about it, right? "

I shrug and force myself to look at him, not at his chin, or his chest, or the exhibit over his left shoulder, but at his eyes, which are slightly almond-shaped. Who knows how he came out that way, his skin darker than mine, his hair bordering on blond. Families sometimes start to look like

15

they have come from other, far-flung places when they stay too many generations in this town. I remember him from high school—his acne, his group of laughing, slouching friends. He stares back an instant, more than an instant—confrontational—and I feel my nerves tensing up, my hand freezing, but I win, because he looks away and asks me, "What?"

Again I shrug. "I know it's ridiculous, but I just don't want to do it."

Jacob drops the vacuum cleaner tube with a clatter.

"At this rate they might as well make me a goddamn professor. Yesterday I had to hand out tests. Today I get to feed the snake."

"You don't *have* to," I tell him, but he walks into the back hall where the mice are caged, so I follow and hand him the can.

"Okay," says Jacob, and because I see he doesn't know how to go about it, I take the can, scoop up a mouse, and give it back.

"Here. It's easy. Now you just drop it in."

We turn to the back of Trance's cage. Jacob is holding the coffee can away from himself as if it contained something explosive; I can hear the mouse skittering inside. I watch his hand, the knuckles tightening, the branching veins. He looks into the can, then wobbles and stretches his free arm out to the wall. I am afraid he will either faint or pretend to faint.

"Never mind, just give it to me," I say, but as I reach out he jerks his arm away and steps back.

"Forget it," he says, and then he has dropped the mouse into the tank and is leaning over it, watching, while I stand looking at the opposite wall. After a minute he claps his hands together and turns to leave.

"Thanks," I say, but he shrugs. The hallway is narrow; to get by he must shimmy past me and the feed barrels as I press against the wall.

"Does it hurt?" he asks after he's made it past me.

"What do you think?" I say. "It would hurt you to get swallowed by a snake, but anyhow she's got to eat."

"No, the work. It's not like you're sitting down all day or anything. It doesn't, I don't know, strain your arm, or whatever?"

"I'm careful."

Jacob looks at the floor and tells me the day-care center needs a worker, just in case I'm looking for a change. His sister-in-law was there, but now she's eight months pregnant.

"Everybody's pregnant," he says. "My sister, my sister-in-law, her friend Kay."

Everybody, I think.

"I'm fine here," I tell him. "I don't mind."

For a moment I imagine he is about to reach out and touch my arm; I'm not sure why. I will it, even, wish his hand against me, but he only examines his palm, runs his fingers through his hair.

"So when are you leaving with your rock band?" I ask, getting back at him.

"We've got to make a demo tape. Once we make that, we send it to this place in Boston that's interested, and then they deal with the bigger places. We figure California in a year or two."

"What do you play?" I ask, and he says, "Everything. Guitar, bass, drums, vocals."

"Everything," I say, my voice sour with disbelief, and Jacob glances through the tanks to the room outside.

"I hate to break up the party," he says, tapping on the glass, "but I've got to finish up that floor."

So there I am, alone in the hall again, and the noise of the vacuum is rising over the tanks, and the mice are nosing each other, scurrying and cramped. Sometimes in high school when I was kissing some boy I would get the extraordinary feeling of departing from my body and hovering above like a chaperon aunt or Peeping Tom, or narrating like a sports announcer, first and second base. Now I do not lose myself in movement. I turn to the right and feel a flash of heat, clench my jaw and feel a tightness. I lace my hands together as if they belonged to two different bodies, but I get nowhere, each hand a twin which knows the other's old routine inside and out.

Then I wonder, what if it all just went away? If I woke one morning, turned my neck and felt nothing, and touched my toes and felt only toes, and swung round sharply, testing, and saw the other side of the room before me, etched and clear? It is hard to remember how I felt before, but mostly it was a question of not noticing—the body no more than a convenient capsule, a reliable vehicle, simply *there*, and I loved to run fast and bend over my fiddle and swim underwater until the pressure sent a buzzing through my head.

Here is what I might do, all in a day, in a morning: buy a car, pack a duffel bag, find a guide to the American Northwest or Southwest, Canada or Mexico. I would move quickly, telling no one of my plans, and while I might buy a tent to keep off rain and bugs, I would not bring a floor mat, the curves of the earth negligible to me—hard angles my pleasure, dissonance nothing to my liquid nerves. Then I would drive, swinging the wheel in wide turns, shifting gears, not on straight highways but on the curving back roads, and it would be summer so I'd be wearing almost nothing, my freckles crowding each other out, each one so anxious to appear.

A square dance begins like a piece of geometry, and you must bow and curtsy and keep the distance right. Then it speeds up, and the caller's voice begins to dip and turn, and the dancers skip a little, leap a little, and if they are agile the speed keeps building until it is not your partner you are dancing with, but the whole square, the whole room even—part of a generous, sliding pattern, like the bees who do this for their life.

At night without my pain I would pitch a tent in a field and sleep over the grass and ants, and some of the ants would crawl on my stomach like streams of water or trail-

18

ing fingers. Or no, there would be real fingers, ten besides
my own, novel and articulate, and the smell of skin and his
knee flung over mine, and something familiar, anything—
Kyra's old blue sweatshirt, my mother's earring, a lacing
from my brace. It is not that I want them there, these
things; they just appear.

The way I will begin is slow, and I'll tell no one but
myself, but waking each day, I'll force myself elsewhere:
India on a camel's back; the Bronx, just for five minutes,
playing basketball with local kids. College, or Kansas City,
or some suburb, pedaling on a bike. The power of sug-
gestion, said my neurologist, is enormous, and so for a
while I watched ballets on television and stared at the hamsters as they ran their wheels. Jacob is tall and brawny, and
when I am thinking of nothing else, his body comes to me
like a possibility that could rub off, a bit of borrowed ease.
He will go to California and play in a rock band; his voice
will soften when he likes what he is doing. In his happiness
he will allow himself to love this historic, well-intentioned
town, but he'll buy himself a house over there, by the sea.

How painful to see people fooling themselves. In my farthest reaches I go where I have no weight, where weight
means nothing—underwater, or on the moon, and I am not
alone, but touching fingers with a ring of bundled astro-
nauts, and we are collecting things in sterile containers to
bring to solid ground. If we can understand this barrenness,
we can understand anything. If we can return from this
weightlessness, we will never be weighed down again. Or I
am alone, so far from the earth that I can watch it spin, so
far from my body that one hand meets the other like a total
stranger, and I greet myself with a new and giddy pleasure,
shaking hands.

HAVE
YOU
SEEN ME?

Willa stood in the patch of light from the open freezer door and watched as the mist climbed in tendrils, swirled and rose. The milk carton in her hands was heavy, its surface smeared with yellowish cream—her mother had made more potato soup. Already the two tall freezers in the basement housed cartons and cartons of soup, enough to last them almost forever—carrot and broccoli soup, soup made of summer and acorn squash, rows of green and yellow frozen rectangles inside the cartons that had once held milk. And on the outsides of the cartons, rows of children—frozen too, their features stiff, their faces etched with frost. *Have You Seen Me? Do You Know Where I Am?* Each time Willa put the cartons in the freezers, she set up the children in pairs so they could have staring contests when she shut the door.

Go on, she thought to Kimberly Rachelle and David Michael, to Kristy-Ann and Tyrone. Stare each other down. She put them boy girl, boy girl, catalogued them by age. Some of the missing children were babies, and these she put on the shelf closest to the bottom. The ones who were eleven, her age, she gave special treatment, tracing their names in the wax coating of the milk cartons with her finger, dusting the frost from their eyes. She could recite their DOBs, their SEXs, HTs, WTs, and EYES, the color of their hair. Willa's mother didn't know about Willa's ordering of the cartons; she was upstairs cooking or painting child after child lined up like soldiers, serious kids in uniforms carrying weapons or naked, puzzled kids looking up at the sky.

Willa's mother expected the end of the world. She donated her paintings to three friends in the town twenty miles down the highway, and they turned them into posters which they hung in the public library and in the windows of the real estate agency that doubled as an art gallery. "You Can't Hug Your Child," they printed in fake child scrawl, "With Nuclear Arms."

Willa thought everyone was overreacting. Sure, there might be silos under the ground and blinking lights that could go off, and escape systems that would lead to nowhere, and broccoli and cauliflower that would grow big as trees afterwards, like in the paintings her mother made. There might be all that, but still what did they know about the end, for she was sure something would survive, making it really not the end at all—maybe only an insect or two, a shiny blind beetle or an ant like the ones in the ant farm her father had given her—some sort of creature, hard, black and shelled, rolling from the rubble like a bead.

She would not go with her mother to the rallies in Chicago and St. Louis, would not wear the buttons and T-shirts or lend her handwriting to the posters. In her room she hung photographs of animals instead of her mother's art work—slow sea turtles and emus with backs like the school janitor's dirty, wide broom. They came from the Bronx Zoo in New York City, the animals on the postcards. Willa's father sent them now and then.

Once a girl in one of her mother's paintings had looked just like Willa, small and dark and suspicious, with the same mess of curly hair. Then Willa had screamed and kicked.

"Take me out of your fucking painting, who said you could paint me? Just take me out!"

"Okay, now stop!" her mother had said, catching Willa by the shoulders. "Just stop screaming and don't go crazy on me. Listen to yourself—listen to yourself, would you just calm down? "

And she had squeezed a big wad of beige paint onto her palette, speared it with a paintbrush, and spread it over the painted Willa's face.

"It wasn't even you," she had said, but Willa had known it was, that her mother had put her there in that lineup of children with puzzled looks, had painted her empty-handed, naked, and puzzled next to an orange boy with wide shoulders and a bow and arrow in his hand. 23

"Just because I say 'fucking' doesn't mean you should," her mother had told her, but then she had kissed Willa's forehead and taken her far down the highway to McDonald's, where Willa ate two hamburgers and drank a thick chocolate shake while her mother drank water and tried not to look at the food.

Underneath their farmhouse was dirt, and underneath the dirt—if not directly underneath, then near enough, her mother seemed sure of it—were silos which were not really silos at all, but this was not Willa's problem. In a movie she saw once, a man drowned in the wheat of a silo, was smothered as the golden grain poured over him like sand, filling up his nostrils and his mouth. She told her mother about it afterwards, the danger of this silo filled with wheat. With *wheat*, Willa had said, which was what silos were supposed to hold.

"Actually silage," her mother had answered. "They're supposed to hold silage—fodder for cows and horses. It must have been a grain elevator."

No, said Willa. It was a silo. She saw it.

"I guess they could do what they wanted—it was only a movie," her mother had said, and then, more thoughtfully, "Hmmm, I suppose it probably happens now and then."

School was one thing, and home alone with her mother was another, and in between were her mother's three friends, who were thin and pretty like her mother and drove out to the house on weekends with bags full of magic markers, envelopes, and petitions that few people in the little town would sign. Sasha was a real estate agent and divorced, and Karen was married and taught kindergarten at Willa's school, and Willa didn't know what Melissa did, except stare sadly at her mother's paintings and say, "Hello, Willa," as if Willa's name were a password or something deserving of the utmost seriousness. Willa's mother gave her three friends homemade bread and sketched their faces on napkins. Sometimes they drank vodka and orange juice and stayed up talking late into the night. When Willa came downstairs in the morning she would find the women sleeping on the couch and floor, still dressed, still wearing rings and necklaces and sometimes even shoes.

At night when no visitors shared the house, Willa's mother told her stories. This had been going on a long time. First it had been her father and mother together. He would say a sentence: "Once there was a truck who lived alone in the Sahara Desert," and her mother would add a sentence: "And he had no glass in his windows and at night the sand came blowing through, and he had no wheels," and her father would add on, and then her mother, each of them perched on Willa's bed, always touching part of her—her knee or her foot, her hand or the small of her back.

Then, when she was seven, her father went to live with a woman he said he had loved in high school, and Willa only saw him twice a year when he left his new family, she left her mother, and they stayed in a hotel in New York and went to museums and the zoo. She always got blisters on those trips from so much walking. After her father left, her mother came home with a whole stack of glossy children's books. Willa couldn't stand the pictures of fat, dimpled children and pets, the stories about going to the dentist, getting a pony, or cleaning up your room.

"*Tell* me one," she would say to her mother, and her mother would try, but she never knew how to start, and the stories stumbled along for a while until Willa grew bored and fell asleep. But over the years her mother improved, or else Willa just grew used to her way of telling. She gave her mother rules: no stories about zoo animals, vampires, or kids named Willa who lived on defunct farms. No stories about the end of the world. Instead, her mother told her more stories about objects—superballs looking for somewhere to bounce, a barn which threw up because of the smelly animals inside it, a snowflake in search of a twin. Sometimes her mother sat at the end of Willa's bed and leaned against the wooden railing. Other times she cupped herself against her daughter and talked right into her ear. Sometimes she slept there all night, squeezed onto the edge of the twin bed. Willa didn't like this, found it sad and embarrassing, though she couldn't say why, but she wouldn't kick her mother out. In winter they stayed warm that way, like pioneers, for the farmhouse was big and drafty in the middle of its field, and the wind came howling round.

After Willa filled the freezer with several loads of soup, she took her book on ants to the kitchen and settled by the wood stove. When the doorbell rang, she didn't look up, too busy with a glossy color photograph of a magnified ant with legs like shaggy black trees. But then her mother came back to the kitchen followed by a girl, or maybe a woman—to Willa the stranger looked young, though she carried a child who hid its face in her coat. Willa's mother showed the girl and baby to the living room, and then she returned to the kitchen and whispered to her daughter that this was a new friend, her name was Melody. They had met at a demonstration in St. Louis; Melody had worked in a nuclear power plant for four years, but now she had quit and was waitressing. She had come to the house for a lesson because she wanted to learn how to draw. Her son was blind and had just turned three.

"It should be fun for you," said her mother after she had called Melody and the child back in. "Isn't he awfully cute?

Would you do us a big favor and watch him while we draw?"

Willa had watched the tiny, silent granddaughter of the farmer down the road while the farmer rode his tractor, but she had never babysat for a blind child, had never met anyone who was blind.

"I don't, I mean—" she said. "I don't really know—"

"Oh listen to you, you're just being modest," said her mother. She turned to Melody. "She's terrific with kids. Already she's babysitting at her age."

"He's pretty much like any other kid, aren't you, Tiger?" said Melody, readjusting the child buried in her arms. "Better, even—he's good as can be. If he wants anything, you can just give a holler. We'll be right upstairs. Or, if you want, we can take him with us."

"I'll watch him," said Willa, for her mother was giving her that look.

When they went up to the studio, her mother and Melody left the child sitting on Willa's baby quilt on the kitchen floor, his back to Willa. For a while she hunched over her book and ignored the boy at her feet, but when she finished the section on carpenter ants, she lifted her head and stared at the child, who had settled on his stomach on the red and yellow quilt. As she stood and leaned over him, she saw that not only was he blind, but he had no eyes, just skin and a row of pale blond lashes where the eyes should have been.

Willa gasped and brought her hands up to her face, then stood for a moment peering into the darkness of her palms, trying to make herself look again. When she lowered her hands, she saw that the boy was sucking his thumb and using the end of his index finger to trace circles on his face. She stared. Did he have eyes under there, so that he wasn't actually blind at all, just confined to a view of his own pale skin? She moved closer to see if she could make out a bulge of eyeball above the fringe of lashes. The skin was smooth and flat like part of a back or stomach—as if nothing were missing, as if eyes had never been invented. Then the boy wrinkled his brow, seemed to be looking at her: Could he see through those eyeless eyes?

He could have been born that way, thought Willa. Not because his mother worked in a nuclear plant, but just because he was born that way. Paula, a fifth grader at school, claimed she had gone to a fair in Florida where they had people like this—Siamese twins joined at the head, children with flippers like dolphins and claws like lobsters, or as hairy as apes. Paula said she had seen the lobster family, three kids and two parents. They were ugly as anything, she said, but they loved each other, that family. They just stood there smiling like goons and holding claws.

As Willa leaned over the child, he reached a hand into the air.

"Ma?" he said.

And she said, "No."

"Can you talk?" she asked, kneeling by him. "What's your name?"

He was perhaps the palest, blondest boy she had ever seen, his hair like milkweed puffs standing straight up on his head, his skin so white you could see veins running underneath it, could see how his blood was blue. He wore a red turtleneck and pink flowered overalls that should have been for a girl. From the way he clenched his fingers to his palms, it seemed he must be angry, or else cold. He did not answer her. As she leaned closer, he reached up and grabbed a fistful of her hair.

"No," she said, starting to unclench his fist with her fingers, but he opened his palm and batted at her curls, swinging them back and forth.

"Girl," he said, and she nodded yes.

He lowered his hand, and she rocked on her heels and looked at him. She could stare and stare, tilt her head to examine him, and it wouldn't matter, for this boy had skin in the place of eyes. He reached out again.

27

"What?" she asked, backing up. His face grew red as if he might begin to cry, though she couldn't imagine where the tears would go.

"What?" repeated Willa, and the boy lifted his arms toward her, so she bent down and scooped him up. He was awkward in her arms, his legs dangling down, but surprisingly light. Willa was used to the house, wore four layers in winter, but this boy's whole body was shaking. With his arms tight around her neck as if he might pull her down, he began, quietly, to sob.

"Oh don't," she said, wanting to drop him and run. "Please don't cry. Don't cry—"

A thread of spittle ran down his chin; perhaps, she thought, his tears flowed like a waterfall down inside his head and out his mouth. She began to circle with him to warm him up, boosting him a little higher each time he threatened to fall.

"This is the kitchen," she told him, and he stopped crying as she went to a bag of onions on the counter and had him touch the brittle skins. She held an onion under his nose, and he batted her hand away. She went to the fridge and pressed his cheek against the side. "Listen," she told him, so he would hear it purr. She took him to the dining room where the table was covered with petitions, posters, and books.

"We don't eat here," she told him. "Usually we eat in the kitchen."

He touched the tabletop and ran his fingers over a copy of a drawing that a Japanese war child had made of its mother. The mother had bright swollen lips; the skin on her hands hung loose like rubber gloves. Willa hated those pictures, had seen that one before and read the caption: HIGASHI YAMAMOTO, MY MOTHER 53 YEARS OLD. Willa's mother had promised to keep them hidden, but sometimes she forgot and left one lying around the house.

"Not for you," said Willa, though she knew he couldn't see it, and she backed up.

28

HAVE YOU SEEN ME?

She brought him to the front room where she used to sit with her mother and father counting trucks in the night, the lights coming toward them on the highway out of nowhere, the rush of sound, then everything growing smaller and smaller, less and less noisy, until it was quiet and they were just sitting there again. In summer they had watched from the porch, and then they could feel the wind of the passing trucks, like feeling the waves the motorboats made when she swam in Lake Michigan on vacations—more ripples than waves, really—and with the trucks it was not quite wind, but more a slight, brief wall of air. Her parents didn't argue when they sat there watching trucks. Her father didn't talk about his office, and her mother didn't talk about the rallies. It was the quietest time they had.

What a baby she'd been in her father's arms, thinking that under the ground was more ground, that in the silos was wheat, that her father would sit there forever in the green stuffed chair. She sat the boy down beside her in the creaking chair and told him to listen for trucks.

"Car," he said, and she said, "A truck is a big car."

"Plane," he said, and she thought of the ones she took to New York to visit her father. The flight attendants always gave her coloring books full of drawings of pilots and suitcases—books meant for much younger kids. Willa knew she should save them for her father's little children, but since he always took her to the hotel, never home, she left the books and crayons on the plane with a wonderful feeling of spite.

He had two children with his new wife, one who was just hers and one who was both of theirs. This meant that Willa had a half-sister and a step-brother, which should have added up to something whole, but though she knew their names were Katherine and William, which was so close to Willa, she had never seen them, not even pictures, and part of her was not convinced they existed. The boy squirmed in her arms, so she put him down and took his hand, but he stumbled, groping at the air, so she picked him up and carried him again, making her way unsteadily to the ant farm in her room.

She couldn't show him, really. She could press his fingers to the glass, but that wouldn't tell him anything, so instead Willa read to him from a library book about army ants, though her ants were simple garden ants. Army ants always moved in columns five ants wide, she told him, marching and marching for seventeen days; then they stopped and laid eggs until they were ready to march again. They had jaws like ice tongs and could eat a leopard, and almost all of them were female. The boy sat in her lap with a mild, interested expression on his face, so she told him about the replete ants who filled their abdomens with nectar until they swelled like grapes, then hung suspended from the ceiling of the nest. When the other ants were hungry, Willa said, they tapped on the mouth of the replete ant, and it spat out a drop of honeydew.

The boy looked a little bored, and he was still shivering, so she lugged him down to the basement where they could be close to the furnace's warmth. As he sat on the floor by the furnace, she kneeled beside him and lightly touched his hair, so like milkweed. How did he get to be so blond, she wondered; his mother had hair as dark as Willa's.

"Stand up, would you," she told him, and when he did she took both his hands and led him slowly across the room. "See, you're not a baby, you're a big boy. You walk fine."

"Fridge," said the boy when they stood before it, for he must have heard it humming, and he reached out and placed his palms flat against the large white door.

"Did you know some children don't live with their parents?" Willa told him. "Either the kids get taken away, kidnapped when they're still young and cute, or else they run away when they're a little older and no one wants them."

Holding the door ajar with her foot, she hoisted him up

and guided his hand to the middle shelf of milk cartons. This was the shelf of the two to five year olds: Jason McCaffrey with blue eyes and brown hair, Crystal Anne Sandors, DOB July 22, 1979, who was three and a half now, pouting like a brat and wearing tiny hoop earrings and pearls. Some of the children had been computer-aged, so that Billy, who was two when he disappeared from his aunt's shopping cart in Normal, Illinois, appeared three years later on the carton as a five year old, his face grainy and stretched-out, coated with wax.

To call those children missing, Willa knew, only meant they were missing for somebody, even though maybe they were found for someone else. Just because they were not at home did not mean they were wandering the earth alone. There were too many of them, just look at all those cartons. First Crystal probably ran into Jeffrey, and then Crystal and Jeffrey ran into Vicki, and soon there were masses of them, whole underground networks. When she went to the supermarket with her mother she spotted them sometimes, kids poking holes in the bags of chocolate in the candy aisle or thumbing through a comic book—kids in matted gray parkas that once were white. They had large pupils and pale skin from living inside the earth.

They knew how to meet underground, these groups of children, knew how to tell a field with a hidden silo from a field of snow, how to comb through the stubble of old corn to find the way down, then slide behind the men in uniforms who guarded the silo like an enormous jewel. They could pass by the waiting dogs, for they were scentless from being frozen for so long. They were thin and coated with wax and could slide quite effortlessly through cracks. Underground they formed squads by age: the blue squad for the nine to eleven year olds, the brown squad for the babies who couldn't walk yet and were covered with mud and dirt. In the underground silos they found piles of wheat and hay left over from the days when the silos had been used on farms. They slept on the hay, woke in the morning with straw stuck in their hair. For breakfast they ground the wheat with stones, formed it into patties, cooked it into small round cakes.

The children knew Willa only as a sort of looming presence. They couldn't see her, but they could feel a shift in the atmosphere when she picked up their cartons, as if a cloud had cast its shadow or a truck swept by the house. They didn't understand how much she made them do; they thought they had their staring contests when they were bored, when really it was Willa pairing them up so they would stare into each other's eyes. Some of them she liked more than others, and these children received favors. The ones who had been there the longest got to sit at the front of the shelf. So far none of them had had to leave. This soup was not for eating. Her mother called it soup for a rainy day.

Someday Willa might have to join them. She did not know how to get there, exactly, but she knew she would figure out a way. Her mother would not be with her, or her father. The larger you were, the harder it was to survive; she could tell that from watching her ants. At eleven, Willa was still quite runty for her age, though her mother made her drink glass after glass of milk. She put the boy down, and then she took out the missing children and told him about each one, placing them in a large ring around him on the concrete floor, as if it were a birthday party and time for Duck Duck Goose. When she got to Craig Allen Denton, REPORTED MISSING FROM THE HOSPITAL ON THE DAY OF BIRTH, 9/11/80, she stopped and stared at him, then wiped the frost from his face with her cuff.

Craig Allen Denton had a shriveled face as white as milk and eyes screwed into slits. His mouth was open in a howl, his fist clenched in a tight ball by his cheek. Willa looked at him again, held him under the light, then turned and stared at the child in her basement. The baby in the picture, she saw, was the toddler on the floor. Melody must have stolen him, or maybe Melody's baby had been switched with him.

32

Before, Willa had thought the baby in the photo had closed his eyes because he was crying. Now she saw that he had no eyes.

Somewhere, to somebody, this eyeless boy was missing. Melody had a son, and the boy had a mother, but still something was wrong. Something was always wrong, no matter how right things seemed. Willa had known this for a while, but still it gave her a headache to think of it. She pulled the boy onto her lap and rubbed her forehead against his hair.

33

"What's your name?" she asked, but he only sneezed.

When she heard a creaking on the stairs, Willa assumed it was a cat. She was showing the boy how to run his fingernail along the side of a carton and gather tiny flakes of wax. She was telling him about Gail May Joliet, DOB 3/12/71, EYES hazel, Gail May who had been computer-aged so that the edges of her face were visible now as a series of small black dots like poppy seeds. "Computer-aged," said the print beneath, and in the wavery lines of her cheeks you could see how they had taken away Gail May's baby fat. Now she looked like a five year old whose cheeks had been carved away.

"She lives in the underground village," Willa told the boy. "She's a gymnast, you should see—she does back flips and balance beam and horse, and I think parallel bars. She's the head of the blue squad. Also she carves tunnels. She's two-and-a-half months older than me."

And she took his hand and placed it over Gail May's face.

Her mother must have been standing there watching from the stairs. She must have been staring at the ring Willa had made of all the soup, of all the milk cartons, arranged not by flavor but by child. She must have been looking at Willa and the boy sitting in the center of the ring. As Willa's eyes lighted on her mother and Melody two steps behind, she tightened her hold on the child.

"What on earth are you doing?" said her mother from the stairs.

Willa shrugged and touched the child's staticky hair. Her mother came toward them, kneeled outside the circle, let out a strained laugh.

"What are you doing with all the soup? It's melting, Willa. Will you just look at that? All my good soup is turning to mush."

34

She was right. Tiny puddles of water were collecting underneath each carton as the soup began to sweat. Her mother started to pick up a carton, but Willa leaned over the boy and swatted at her hand.

"Leave it, Mom, okay? I'll clean it up."

"I thought you were reading in your room," said her mother. "We heard you reading to him."

She stepped over the cartons, scooped the boy up, handed him up to Melody, and whispered something. Then Melody and the boy disappeared up the stairs. Outside the ring of cartons, Willa's mother crouched.

"Were you building a city?" she said. "There are blocks in the attic if you want to build with him. Why did you have to defrost all my soup?"

If she had felt like it, she could have explained things logically to her mother, how in an Emergency Situation the radiation would seep into the basement, inside the furnace, inside the canned goods, stacks of magazines, bottles of wine. How it would go right through the thick white insulation of the fridge, through the wax and cardboard of the milk cartons, through all those dotted faces to the soup.

But her mother knew that, and still she kept making soup.

Willa sighed. "I wasn't defrosting."

"What were you doing then?"

Her mother stepped over the cartons and kneeled by her side.

"Just playing."

"Well then," said her mother. "I'll put them away. I can't have all that soup melting. You can't refreeze, it doesn't work."

"I'll do it," said Willa, and as her mother sat cross-legged in the middle of the circle, she began collecting the cartons by age, by group, starting with the babies and moving up.

"Melody has potential as an artist," said her mother. She handed her daughter a carton, out of order.

"I'll do it. Let me do it." Willa peered at the carton—G. Phillip Stull, red squad—then put it back on the floor.

"Oh—oh I see," her mother said. "You were talking to him about these pictures, weren't you? You were telling Melody's baby about the children on the cartons."

Willa continued her ordering.

"I think a lot of it is media panic, honey," her mother said. "I mean, from what I've heard. A lot of these kids are with their divorced parents, or there's a custody problem, or they ran away. You'd be surprised. Most of them aren't actually missing at all."

Willa turned and began to collect the two to four year olds.

Upstairs, she went to Melody, who was cutting an apple into pieces in the kitchen, and stood by her side. In the living room she could hear her mother murmuring to the child.

"Hi there," said Melody, and Willa said hi.

"Your Mom said I could cut Jo-Jo an apple. Thanks for playing with him. Did he give you any trouble?"

Willa shook her head. Melody popped a slice of apple into her mouth and chewed.

"He's a good kid. All his babysitters love him, once they get used to him."

"Did he, I mean, was he—"

"He was born like that."

Willa nodded, and Melody squinted at her. "Has your mother been telling you stuff? About where I worked and all?"

Willa shook her head.

"Oh, okay. It's just that I've had a bunch of jobs, worked

all over the place, but my last job was at that power plant down by Acton, and it's hard to say, about his eyes. You can never say for sure, but if your mother told you I shouldn't take any more chances with that place, I can't argue. Too many funny things."

"What'd you think when he was born?"

Melody shook her head. "I had a C-section—you know, when they cut you open?" She traced a line down her stomach. "I was out cold."

"So you didn't see him."

"Oh sure, I saw him. They bring them in. I was real happy, seeing him there. I was—I guess I was so drugged out or something, but I just kept waiting for him to open up his eyes, you know?"

"He's got such blond hair," said Willa.

"His daddy's a towhead." Melody leaned toward Willa and whispered confidentially. "I'm blond, too, really," she said, lifting a lock of her dark hair, "but not white blond like him, more washed out, kind of dirty blond. Now you've got a real pretty color. That's all natural, huh?"

Willa nodded, and Melody smiled a crooked smile which almost looked sad. Then she touched the tip of Willa's nose with an outstretched finger.

"Lucky you. Hang onto that hair, okay?"

She scooped the rest of the cut apple into her hand, tossed the core into the garbage can, and walked away.

When Willa went to the living room, she saw Melody on the floor with the boy. They were playing the game where his mouth was a tunnel, the apple a chugging train. Jo-Jo was laughing and had his fingers splayed across his mother's face. Willa stood in the doorway, a sour feeling in her gut.

"I hate to say it, but we've got to get going," Melody said to her mother.

And her mother answered, her voice quick and concerned. "So soon, but you just got here. You hardly drew at all."

"They say the weather won't hold out." Melody looked up at the ceiling as if it were the sky. "We have a drive."

Willa's mother came and stood with her while Melody lay Jo-Jo on his back and zipped him into a snowsuit. Then she and her mother moved to the front door and watched Melody pick her way down the slippery stairs with the boy on one hip, a knapsack on her back, her drawings in a roll under her arm.

37

"You two take care now, okay?" said Melody, turning when she reached the bottom step, and Willa smiled a quavering, forced smile. Melody strapped Jo-Jo into a car seat that looked like an elaborate plastic bubble, slid into the driver's seat, and sat there a moment warming up. The car was blue and rusty, coughing as if the air were too much for it, but after a minute Melody waved. Then she and Jo-Jo drove away.

"Why couldn't they have stayed longer?" Willa asked after the car and then the sound of the car had disappeared. "I have nobody to play with."

"I don't know, honey," said her mother, and her voice sounded tired and disappointed. "People have things to do."

Willa went to her room and lifted the cardboard shield which tricked her ants into thinking they were underground. They froze for an instant, then saw it was just Willa and continued on. Their paths were so easy to follow; she could see through the glass on both sides and watch their every move. She would let them go, she decided. Not now, when the ground was frozen, but in spring when the earth grew soft and they could burrow down. She would take the farm outdoors, crack open its sides, and let the ants spill out like beads.

But then Willa remembered the Queen ant, the one who had broken off her own wings when she settled in the farm to lay her eggs, who lived off the energy of her useless flight muscles, leaving the broken wings in a corner of the farm. Auto-amputation was what they called it in *The Wonder World of Ants*. Willa had wanted to get rid of those wings, hated looking at them, but she couldn't reach them without dismantling the farm. The Queen couldn't fly, and she was too fat to walk. Out in the world, abandoned by her guards and workers, she would die.

Willa wished her ants were leafcutter ants, the kind who dragged bits of plants and caterpillar droppings to their underground nests and grew fungus on them, like farmers. Then they ate the fungus and fed it to their kids. That was practical—the leafcutters could live through almost anything, but Willa's ants were used to bread and honey and being fed by her. The missing children, the way she saw them, were more like leafcutter ants. Somehow they knew how to get by.

Ants had survived on this earth for more than a hundred million years. It didn't surprise her. The smaller you were, the better your chances. Her mother made her drink milk so she would grow big and strong and so there would be cartons for the soup. But big and strong was the wrong thing; small was what you had to be. She would not drink milk anymore. In the end, if it came to that, she would find a friend like Jo-Jo. Underground he would shine in his paleness like the fireflies in summer in the fields out back. Blind, Jo-Jo would be able to sense corners, the twisted workings of the paths, and if she took his hand, he would guide her far from the silos, deep into the insulated center of the earth.

YELLOW
TENT

From the shore, the way the dusk blurred edges, he might have taken her for something caught in the rubble of the stream. She could have been a log, or an alligator if it had been the tropics, or an animal carcass heavy with water resting against a fallen branch. In fact, she was a girl, quite alive and stretched in the Black River with her arms above her head, clinging hard to a bit of tree. Darren knew the shape was Meg because he had followed her down to the river and stood pretending not to look as she peeled off her T-shirt and shorts. Watching her lift her shirt above her head, he had experienced a moment of panic, first at expecting flesh, then at seeing that suit there like the mottled skin of a beast.

"Do you like it?" she had asked. "My six dollar bargain basement jungle suit."

As he watched, she had lowered herself into the river, first up to her ankles, then her calves, and then she was lying on her back in the shallow middle, holding onto a branch so the current wouldn't pull her away. Darren sat on shore hugging his knees, aimed two flashlights across the water and watched as their beams began to waver, refracted by the stream. As it grew darker he aimed them at Meg, a spot on each of her cheeks, on each of her breasts, then lower where his *Encyclopedia of the Human Body* said her two twin ovaries would be. He loved that word: ovaries. He had memorized Woman on the page, decided to be a doctor like his father so he could know more, touch the places that made and maintained life—ovaries, but also hearts, kidneys, lungs. He would cup a heart still beating in his hand, learn not to be squeamish about blood.

I am camping, he thought, with a girl. I am helping her escape.

He was good at it, this aiming of the lights, just as he was good at hammering nails in tricky places and at building model ships. His father had told him that with such steady hands he could be a surgeon. He picked a spot to focus on—her nose, her eyes, those ovaries, and there, the breasts again—and saw to it that the circles of light landed just where he had decided they should go.

But now she was rising from the river, impossible to pinpoint, a large, dark shape. Darren's lights went dancing in search of their moving target, then spread out on the surface of the water, lost.

"What?" her voice asked.

He lit her face. "Huh?"

She put her hand in front of her eyes. "What're you doing with those flashlights?"

He shrugged. "Fooling around."

In one quick motion she had wrapped herself in a dark towel, her arms crossed protectively against her chest.

"Yeah, well quit shining them at me, if you don't mind."

He lowered the lights to the ground.

"Give it," she said, but he pulled away.

"I need mine. I brought one for each of us."

"Okay, so give me mine."

She grabbed the light and turned it on him, shone it straight into his eyes so he was forced to look away. When he looked back, she was covered with free-floating blue spots. Darren shielded his eyes with his hands.

"How do you like it?" she asked. "Fun, huh?"

"Sorry," he mumbled, peering through his fingers.

"I could aim it other places, too," she said. "But I wouldn't stoop so low."

At the campsite they sought ground, flat ground unmarred by tree roots, rocks, and twigs, and when they found

40

a spot, they stretched the canvas out in a tight yellow square. As she crouched at one corner and he knelt diagonally across, they took the poles and worked them through the cloth, then pushed the stakes into the soft dirt. After the tent arched its back and rose, they moved away with their flashlights and examined it—so yellow in the scrubby campground, so puffed and artificial, a hothouse blossom in a bed of weeds.

They were cousins, Meg only twenty but already leaving her new husband. "I need you to help me," she had told him on the phone. And because he was fourteen, and it was summer, he had said yes, okay, he would leave his father a note. On the small roads winding south toward the Ozarks, she had rewarded him by letting him drive. It had not been Meg, but Darren who picked out food when they stopped along the way, and Darren who pumped gas and washed the windows of the rusty car. She had sat in the passenger's seat with her chin in her hand, still and quiet, staring out. He had chosen a campground, pleased to wield power, but Meg, looking out the window, had said it was no good—too crowded—and the second one he picked was too deserted and gave her the creeps. Finally they had found this place, equally deserted off some long dirt road near the Black River.

"We have to see the river," she had said, "before we pitch the tent."

Darren had no sisters, and he went to an all boys' private school, so just sitting in a car with an older girl, a woman, just kneeling across from her as she stretched the canvas of the tent and ran her palms over the ground feeling for bumps—just this was enough to make him crack his knuckles and feel a tightness in his scalp. And then this was Meg, his rebel cousin, the one who had only gone to junior college and had married at nineteen—her husband named, of all things, Moses, the owner of an organic farm, a tall, handsome, stuttering fellow who grew cabbages the size of watermelons and watermelons the size of pigs. Darren had not been invited to the tiny wedding, but he had gone to visit them for a weekend a few months later when his father was at a cardiology conference in the East.

It hadn't been what he expected, not an adult house where his cousin Meg was changed into something warm, solid, and predictable like his Aunt Leona or Aunt Kay. Meg and Moses lived two hours from St. Louis in an enormous, tired old farmhouse—room upon nearly empty room, each bestowed with one or two objects as if to indicate its purpose, so that Darren had felt as if he were wandering through the barren music rooms and libraries of his board game Clue—a guitar on the floor of one room, some books in crates in another, a third room peopled with Meg's old stuffed animals and china dolls. This, he had thought, is where they'll put the baby when they have one. The wall above the fireplace in the living room was covered with small discolored squares where photographs of a family must have once hung. Meg and Moses had bought the house from an old farmer who was moving in with his daughter. The penciled heights of children ran up the bathroom door.

Meg had worn a limp green dress printed with a pattern of forks and spoons and hugged him hard when he arrived, then put on a tape of some woman crooning about Paris. Moses had shown up later bearing a crate of peas from his greenhouse, and they had shelled peas on the front porch steps, plinking them into tin pots, saying nothing at all until the music stopped short in the middle of a song. Then Meg asked Moses to please flip over the tape. For dinner they had eaten peas on top of sticky rice and watermelon for desert. At night, sleeping on the floor of an empty room, Darren had listened hard for noises that might teach him something, but it had been so quiet, with only the hum of the refrigerator and the cicadas outside competing to be heard.

And now by the tent he watched his cousin disappear for a moment with her backpack and return dressed in shorts

42

and a T-shirt, holding her wet bathing suit away from her
like a smelly fish. He watched her hang the suit from a tree
and dive into the tent and push into her sleeping bag and lie
still as a mummy—so swift, that chain of movements. Darren followed behind and climbed into his own sleeping bag,
the one he had gotten for a Boy Scout trip when he was ten.
It was covered on its flannel inside with men hunting and
men fishing and men standing with walking sticks by
snow-capped mountains. But the men by the mountains
looked more like angels, really, the way the snowcaps
hovered behind their shoulders like broad white wings.
That had always bothered Darren, for he knew the sleeping
bag people hadn't meant it that way. Now he wanted to tell
his cousin, to peel back his sleeping bag, shine the light and
show her the awkward men with jeans and guns and stiff
wings. She might lean over to see, nestle her chin against
his shoulder, hold him there.

43

Once Meg had held him for hours. She probably didn't
remember, and if she did, she doubtless didn't think he remembered. But once, right after his mother died and he had
decided not to talk to anyone until he thought of something
worthwhile to say, Meg had shown up with Aunt Leona,
her mother, to help out. Darren had been seven, Meg thirteen, her dark hair stringy and down to the small of her
back, her wrists covered with bright string bracelets she
had woven herself. No one had known what to do with
Darren. He ate all his meals and washed himself and went
to bed on time, but he would not speak—not for two weeks,
not one word—and if you tried to touch him, he scratched
like a startled cat.

Meg had tickled him, snuck up as he crouched in the
sandbox in the backyard and covered his eyes from behind,
then gone for his pale and tender belly and the soles of his
feet until he was helpless with laughter and then tears. She
had held him for a long time. She had not been big, not like
his mother, but hard and strong as a boy, and when his nose
had begun to run she had wiped it with her sleeve and

kissed his face with her hard mouth and told him to keep crying—it was good for him, she cried all the time, and she was already thirteen. This information he had received with mild disgust: thirteen and still always crying.

But then he had closed his eyes and pretended she was his mother, though she did not feel right, and when they went back inside he had begun to talk again—small words, careful words. His father had asked Meg to explain exactly how she had achieved such good results. That night Darren had crawled under her quilt in the living room, and she had held him until she fell asleep. The next morning, he remembered, she wouldn't comb her hair, hadn't combed it for days; it hung in elaborate tangles down her back.

44

"Rat's nest," Aunt Leona had called it, catching Darren in her arms and pinning him against her so she could run a comb wetted with water through his own short, glossy bangs. "See how Darren lets me," his aunt had said, and from across the room Meg had sneered, sucking on a lock of her black hair.

And now, in the tent, either she was sleeping or else she did not want to talk to him, hardly two words since the river, though when she did talk her tone was bright and cheerful, as if nothing at all were wrong. A dim annoyance began to push its way through him that he had come all this way, been so helpful, and now it was like camping with a stone. He coughed, turned onto his stomach, then onto his back. He swatted at a fly which circled above him, buzzing louder each time its circuit brought it past his ears. A grown man, he knew, would either not be bothered by a fly, or else would reach out with his large hand and intercept it in the dark. But the noise of the fly was making Darren grit his teeth, or was it that the surrounding silence was made still quieter by this circling buzz? Darkness itself was too thick in the low-ceilinged tent, the air hot and close.

"Meg?" He said it softly first. "Hey, Meg?"

She stirred, turned toward him slightly. He drew in his breath. "There's a fly in here."

Her voice when she spoke was wide awake. He knew, then, that she too had been lying there listening. "If we open the flap," she said, "more might get in."

"I know. But it's hot in here, huh?"

"Sleep on top of your sleeping bag if you're too hot." Her voice was level, sane, adult in a way which annoyed him. They were supposed to be equals here, the way they had shared the driving, the way she had called on him for help.

45

"But aren't you hot?" he asked.

He wanted her to ease her long body out of the sleeping bag and lie on top of the fabric where she would be closer to him, where he could brush her leg in pretended sleep. He wiggled out of his bag, felt her next to him as he rearranged his legs. He was still wearing his jeans, hot and sticky against his skin.

"My jeans are roasting," he said.

He could hear her sigh. "Then take them off."

"Yeah, but my shorts are in the car."

"So sleep in your undies, Darren. I won't look."

He couldn't do that, knew how slight his body was in his baggy white briefs, how flat his buttocks, how narrow his hips—knew, also, how he would wake in the morning with an erection.

"Are you glad you left Moses?" he asked abruptly, astonished at the question, which left his mouth before he had time to consider it. Actually he didn't really care, just wanted her to talk to him, wanted to know if she remembered holding him that day.

"I didn't *leave* Moses," she said. "I'm just taking a trip."

Something sank inside him: this was not what she had said before. Before they had been fleeing, leaving, getting away from. Trips went in circles, away from home and back; he and Meg had been going in a line.

"You said you wanted to leave him," Darren told her.

He could feel her turn toward him in the dark, how the whole atmosphere shifted as if switching axes. Now she was talking to him, not past him, not on the way to sleep, but away from it. Now, finally, they were together in the tent.

"Did you like him?" she asked, and her voice was tight.

"Moses?"

"Yeah. I mean, you only saw him a little, but what'd you think?"

He panicked: Say something good and she will disagree. Say something nasty and she will bristle the way people always do when you insult their families, even if they do it plenty themselves.

He made his voice neutral and flat. "He seemed nice."

Her breath was close to him. "He is nice. Did he seem—I don't know—very adult to you?"

He didn't know what she meant by this. "No, I mean, not like my dad or something. But he seemed kind of . . . serious."

"He *is* serious. He's so serious—you're right. He's serious about his plants and me and the car."

"How come the car?"

"He washes it once a week—that old pile of rust. I don't know . . . he wants me to have babies. Babies, Jesus, Darren. Can you imagine?"

He could. He knew where her ovaries were, thought it was a wonderful, a tremendous thing that she could make a baby inside of her, but not with that Moses who stuttered and would raise a child as if it were a special kind of fruit.

"Don't you want to have kids?" he said.

Her voice was quick and agitated. "Someday, sure, I guess. Really I could go either way. But, I mean, I don't know, lately I've been thinking—my God, I mean I still forget to feed the cat . . ."

She trailed off. He thought perhaps she was about to cry. Then he could lean over and comfort her, the way she had comforted him. But when she started up again, her voice had swung around in a different direction, far from tears.

"Let's just have fun, okay?"

"Okay," he said, though he had no idea what she intended.

"Let's—" She paused to think. "Let's tell ghost stories. I can't sleep with that goddamn fly. You start."

He didn't know how to tell ghost stories, had always been the one at Boy Scouts to listen, not talk, but he had to think of something now for Meg, or else she would roll over and go to sleep. There was one about a man with a saw for an arm who came down to a girls' camp to cut trees, then to cut legs and arms, until eventually just the blond head of a girl was left rolling around like a basketball, screaming "Timber! Timber!" as a warning in the night. For hours after he had been told that story, Darren had lain awake hearing a shrill voice calling Timber out to no one, seeing a forest littered with girls' parts. But he had to tell Meg something, and this was the only one he remembered from beginning to end.

47

"Okay, so once there was this big forest, and a lumberjack guy lived up there all alone—"

"Ooooh," she said.

"And in an accident he lost his arm and tied on a saw instead."

"Oh shit—I know this one."

"You tell it then."

"But you know it too, Darren—there's no point. Anyhow I hate that story. Don't you know another?"

"No."

They were silent for a long moment. He could feel her disappointment. Then her breathing grew more regular, as if she might fall asleep.

"We could toast marshmallows," he suggested and pushed closer to her until his leg was leaning against her sleeping bag.

"We could, but we need a fire. It's too late to build a fire. We have no wood."

"We could make marshmallow taffy with our fingers."

She laughed. "Oh yeah, we used to do that at camp. That was fun. Isn't it a little dark?"

"Naw." He felt expert, in control. He would show her entertaining things, take her mind off her troubles. He sat up to rummage for the marshmallows, which he knew were in a bag near his feet. "We have the lights."

They sat, Meg still in her sleeping bag, Darren in his jeans on top of his bag. He handed her two marshmallows, took two for himself. With the flashlights propped nearby, they squished and worked at the candy, stretched it out until it hung in smooth white ribbons between their hands.

"God, I wish I was your age," Meg said between mouthfuls.

"You're crazy. I wish I was your age."

"Oh no you don't. When I was thirteen—"

"Fourteen."

"When I was fourteen I just ran around in the woods all day with this other girl, Charlotte. We didn't give a shit about anything—school, other people, boys. We had a whole pretend town out there—a store, a bar, a beauty parlor, a fast-food place. It was amazing."

"When you were *my* age?" She had seemed so old. He couldn't imagine how she had played such baby games.

"Why, what do you do for fun, big shot?" she asked.

"I dunno."

"Run around with girls?" Her voice was teasing, close to being cruel, he thought, though he wasn't sure. She nudged him with her elbow, her taffy-covered hand held aloft in the air. The batteries, he thought. They might run out if we keep the flashlights on too long.

"Well, don't go and get married," she said. "Promise me you won't get married until you're at least fifteen."

"Okay."

"Not that it's a bad thing, marriage. I'm not saying that."

"No."

"It's not that I'm unhappy, Darren. Please don't go telling your dad I'm totally miserable or something. They all already think I'm out of my mind."

"I don't."

"Thanks." She coughed. "Moses is thirty. Did you know that?"

"No."

"He doesn't look thirty, though, does he? Skinny men never look their age until later. You'll look about twenty when you're thirty, too. He never had a real relationship before me. Women were scared of him, I think. I—he says I discovered him. *Discovered*, like he's a country and I'm Columbus, you know?"

She giggled, but her voice, when she spoke again, was sober.

"He doesn't stutter when we're alone together, never trips up. What an amazing thing, like I could cure him or something, only as soon as we're around other people, he starts up again. I *hate* it when he does that. I just sit there and bite down on my tongue. Isn't that awful?"

Darren switched off the flashlights, brought his sticky hand to his mouth and began cleaning his fingers with his tongue. He was starting to feel tired, his head drooping toward the worn cotton of his sleeping bag. Her voice was animated. He could picture their tent from outside, from up above—how until he had switched the lights off it had glowed a deep yellow, and you could see shadows in it—hands waving, heads leaning, his blond head and her darker one looking the same from out there. And then with the lights out, how the whole thing had almost disappeared—maybe a dim hump in the middle of the grove now, a haystack or a bulky sleeping animal. Maybe nothing at all.

"Damn stupid fly," she said. "Still buzzing around. Do you hear it?"

He murmured something like a yes.

"Are you sleeping, Darren?"

And then it was she who was leaning toward him, searching out his face, tweaking his ear.

"First you get me all awake, and then you fall asleep on me. Thanks a lot."

His hand as he pushed it through the dark caught hers

just as it was retreating. First he swatted, as if to rid himself of her, but then he closed his hand around three of her fingers and held them aloft in the air. They weren't sticky, her fingers. They were long and smooth; she must have cleaned the taffy with her tongue. He wanted her to touch his hair, to press her fingers to the roots and smooth backwards, cup his head inside her hands. He would hold on to her fingers, keep her there until he was sure she wouldn't go away.

"What? " she said, her voice gentle, perplexed. He brought her hand down back by his head, guiding it, and for an instant she stroked his hair away from his forehead, just as he was praying she would do.

"You should go to sleep," she said.

"You should go to sleep," he mimicked in a whisper.

But it was as if she were ironing his hair, smoothing it back over his skull, over and over again with her palm. He didn't know what she was at that moment, what he wanted her to be. He was breathless at the blurriness of it—how maybe he was sleeping and maybe he wasn't, how maybe it was a mother's hand, or a cousin's, or a sister's, or something else. He could live forever on the edges of such boundaries, didn't want to change a thing.

But then he found himself turning over on his stomach, for it was her neck, the hollow there where he could feel her bones, that his mouth most wanted, and her mouth with its taffy smell. He ran his hands along her face, tunneled toward her through the dark. How long she was, though he could not see her, her skin with its scent of musty river and damp leaves. His hands were not his hands, but something run away from him, two live animals burrowing through her sleeping bag, pushing past her T-shirt to her skin.

"Darren! " she said, her voice sharp in his ear, so close her breath heated his face. She sat up, pushing him away by his shoulder as she groped around.

"Where's that flashlight? " she asked.

"What?"

"The flashlight. Would you just give me the stupid flashlight?"

It was at his feet, he knew that. He pointed in the darkness, then realized she couldn't see his arm.

"Find it, Darren." He could hear her draw in her breath. "Please."

He handed it to her and she shone it at him, not right in his eyes but just below, so that it lit up his whole face.

"What the hell are you thinking?" she said. "I mean, what—do I have to go sleep in the car?"

He turned his face away from her, toward the wall of the tent. You started it, he wanted to tell her. The way you lay there in the water, asked me about girls, invited me out camping in the first place. The big deal you made about your stupid bathing suit.

He was about to cry, he knew he was, could feel his throat constrict, his nostrils flare. Every place in his body that had been fluttering a moment ago felt heavy now, his hair itchy and sticky, the marshmallow taste in his mouth turned pasty thick. He turned his face back to the light. He would say he was sorry, though he was not—anything to get over the moment and make her be nice again.

But his cousin was pushing herself out of her sleeping bag, unzipping the flap of the tent, and then she had disappeared into the dark.

Go after her, he told himself. If you don't go after her she might take the car, and then you'll be left alone. He could imagine her doing that; there was something crazy about her almost, the way she swung about like that, stroking his hair one second, yelling at him the next. Crazy, he thought. Nuts. The whole family said so. She had been crazy to marry Moses and crazy to call up Darren out of nowhere and now she was just as crazy to go back, for he knew she would go back and live with her husband in that enormous empty house.

"Meg?" he called, and then again, but she did not answer.

Stepping barefoot through the flap and onto the pine-needled ground was almost like stepping into day. Outside the air felt lighter, easier to breathe; he could make out tree trunks, a garbage can, and farther off, the car. As he approached he saw her sitting on the hood, knees tucked up, arms wrapped around herself, crying. Not the way he thought a woman would cry, but dry, heaving sobs like his father's years ago. Darren went and stood by her. He knew he must not touch her, not so much as put his hand upon her knee. At first she didn't notice him, but after a few minutes she looked up and made a grimace he thought might be a smile through her tears.

52

"Poor Darren, you should have gone camping with your friends, huh? That would have been more fun. You know how I remembered you?"

He shook his head.

"I remembered this totally sweet, withdrawn little kid with a runny nose. Hardly a kid at all, more like a little grandfather. I wanted—" Her voice snagged. "I guess I just wanted to hang out with my little cousin, you know? Like how we played catch, after—when your mom died, do you remember?"

He nodded, though he didn't remember.

"I know I forced you to. Probably it was awful of me, the way I stuck you in the yard and threw that ball at you until you had to do something, or you'd get all smashed up in the face. But then you started playing, counting how many times you could catch it. You liked it eventually, didn't you? Anyhow you wouldn't stop."

As she peered into his face, he felt something contract in his stomach again.

"Everyone thought I was being nice to you, but really I was just making you play. I'm sorry. I should take you home. I should go home."

"In the morning," he said.

"Okay, but then go to sleep now, or I'll really feel like a jerk."

"What about you?"

"I—" She waved her hand in the air. "I'll just sit."

"There are bugs."

"I've seen worse."

He swallowed hard, then whispered. "I don't want to be in there alone."

He wanted to remind her of how she had held him. He didn't know about playing catch, couldn't remember it; perhaps she had made it up. Maybe he had invented his memory of her tickling him in the sandbox and holding him in the living room that night.

His hands were creeping toward her knees, couldn't help it, his fingers toying with the frayed edge of her shorts.

"Stop," she said, digging her nails hard into his skin. She shimmied backwards on the hood until she was crouched by the windshield. When she spoke, her voice was so firm he could not disobey.

"Go," she said. "Turn around, get back in that tent, and go to sleep."

On bare feet calloused from summer, he pivoted and took quick steps away from Meg, over the uneven, needled ground. A little grandfather, she had said, but he would still be young when she was old. Already she was old—the way her face had crumpled when she cried. As he climbed through the flap and into the sleeping bag, he heard her crying again, those rough, trapped sobs as if something were scrambling up the walls inside her throat.

In his mind Darren rocked her the way he was sure she had rocked him; he smoothed her forehead, pressed down on her temples and eyelids, untangled the knots in her hair. Then he went further, though it would make her cry still harder if she knew. Inside Meg were hidden parts. He traced his thoughts along the black lines of uterus and cervix, rectum, fallopian tube, anus and urethra—along that curved cleft marked cervical canal. If nobody knows, he thought, it can't be a bad thing, and so in his mind he touched his cousin outside too—her breasts and the dip of her hips and between her legs and the throat which was rasping now, then quieter, then silent outside the tent. In the sleeping bag covered with winged hunters, he pulled off his jeans and touched himself as if he were his cousin. He was almost tall enough, his skin was almost soft enough.

Tomorrow he would offer to drive, and she would let him. Probably she would fall asleep in the car. He could take her anywhere then. He could take her anywhere, but he would take her home. Moses would come to the porch, and he and Meg would hug and begin again, at least for a little while. It was not the right thing—Darren knew this—but it would happen, for it was only a trip they were on—out somewhere, then back. Soon Meg would have a baby, she and Moses, and then another.

Part of him wanted to stay in the woods with Meg. There he might grow older, she younger, until they met on a sort of middle ground. It wouldn't matter, then, that she was his cousin, married and twenty, and he fourteen. In the woods they would live like animals. His tent would grow tattered and fall, but it wouldn't matter; they would serve as each other's tents. If she would protect him, he would protect her. That would be fair.

But he couldn't get her to lie next to him, not even for one night. Women were like that, they slipped away. He'd heard his father say it in a confident, gravelly voice, how women slipped away. Darren had agreed, acting older than his years. "I know," he'd said. And here, alone, he did.

THE
BLUE
HOUR

The pretty little night nurse Juanita takes all the Get Well cards, punches holes in them, and strings them on a ribbon around the room. They flap whenever somebody comes in. The day nurse has no time for anything, all business and scrubbed, efficient hands. Juanita has a baby, six months old, and she shows me his picture shyly, cups it in the palm of her hand where I cannot see it, then slowly, ceremoniously, turns her wrist. There: her son, framed by her fingers, fat and brown in his starched and ironed clothes. At night, though it is against regulations, she opens my window halfway to let in air. Then the cards touch covers in the breeze like a row of lightly clapping hands. People I hardly remember are sending me those cards: *Best Wishes, Heard You Were Under the Weather, May You Be Up and Around.*

"You have many friends, no?" Juanita says.

"I guess so," I say, though I am not sure at this point, for I have hardly any visitors, just this growing strip of cards.

Once in a story I heard somewhere, an old woman took some of her husband's ashes and put them in an egg timer, saying that he might as well do some work now that he was dead, having been a lazy oaf his whole life. I tell Juanita while she sponges me, and she says not to talk of such things, to be cheerful.

"I am cheerful," I say. "It's a funny story."

"One two three, turn," says Juanita, and she flips me over as easily as if I were a baby and begins to clean my back.

I am not dying. This is what they tell me: "You're a

strong and resilient lady, Mrs. Haven, and with a little rest you'll be out of here in no time."

They are making two mistakes—first, I am no longer a Mrs., and second, I am nearing my seventy-seventh birthday, and though it is true I do not feel as if I am dying, I cannot quite imagine what other event might be taking place. My symptoms, I am almost embarrassed to admit, are nearly pleasurable; I feel small, continual palpitations in my chest, legs, and arms, as if a crew of gentle carpenters were tapping with rubber hammers on my bones. Also, I cannot get up. My legs buckle under me and the world spins black and gold before my eyes, but it is a giddy spinning and I quite enjoy it, so that sometimes I raise myself up halfway just to get the beginning of the spin. The doctors say it is circulatory and heart trouble coupled with depression and exhaustion. They ask me if I live alone. I do not mind the hospital, not at night when Juanita is there. During the day I mind it terribly, and become, for the profit of the day nurse, a wretched, crotchety old hag.

Here is Juanita when she comes to work: a small girl, twenty-five last June, and she wears a coat passed down from her sister, black with a red collar and a Christmas brooch on the lapel. She always stops in my room first before she passes on to the nurses' station to leave her coat and purse. She would like to wear red fingernail polish, but the nurses are told not to be showy, so Juanita sneaks by with a pale coral. Her mother, she tells me when I ask, is Puerto Rican; her father is from New York. She has a tiny accent which gives curves to her words, but she has named her baby Robert James and has no interest in cultivating ethnicity. Her husband works as a postman, not an easy job, she tells me—such pressure to move fast, and he has scars on his hands and legs from attacks by neighborhood dogs. Around her neck she wears a green jade heart and a locket on a thin gold chain.

"I have another story for you," I tell her, and she wags her finger and says, "Tell me happy, only happy stories, or else you'll make me cry."

So I tell her about the time, as a young woman ushering at the theater, I found a pearl and gold bracelet wedged in the crack of a velvet seat. I turned the bracelet in at the box office and in three months nobody had claimed it, so I took it home.

57

"Yes?" she says, her hands busy dropping pills into fluted paper cups.

"I wore it," I tell her, "for three years. It was a beautiful— it is a beautiful bracelet. But every time I wore it I expected someone to come running up to me and tell me it was theirs. I was nervous all the time, pulling down my cuff. You can't imagine."

"You could have left it home," she says sanely. She places the paper cups on a tray before me, and I begin to swallow between sentences, the blue and amber pills vanishing one by one.

"Anyway, one day it really happened. I was walking up an aisle in the market, buying vegetables, and a young woman ran up, grabbed my wrist, and said, 'excuse me, but I think that's my bracelet you're wearing.'"

"It was hers!" says Juanita.

"She said it was hers, and I believed her—why wouldn't I believe her? Only you know what?"

She shakes her head almost imperceptibly, and when I wait for more of a reaction, shakes it harder until the red hoops in her ears begin to sway.

"It wasn't hers and never had been. She was trying to, you know—pick me up."

"My God," says Juanita, her hand flying to her mouth to suppress a giggle.

"But I didn't understand, and so you know what I did? I gave her the bracelet, and then, as a reward for my finding it, she took me out to dinner."

Juanita is perched on my bed, leaning toward me. Her

eyes dart to her watch, and she draws in her breath and straightens up.

"It's time for Mr. Feldman in 309. Tell me quick, how did the lady know it was lost? She must—"

"Wait—I'm getting there. So she took me to a very fancy French restaurant, and halfway through dinner, she told me it wasn't her bracelet at all."

She rolls her eyes. "So how come she knew it was lost?"

"She says she just made it up—a lucky guess. Charlotte was smart that way. Maybe she saw me playing with my cuff?"

Juanita looks at her watch and gasps. "I've got to go—"

"Anyway, I let her keep the bracelet."

She makes a tsk sound. "Oh, I would like to see it."

"You would, would you?" I say. I have been storing this up all week; it will make her stay a minute more. "Charlotte died last year and left the bracelet to me. I want to give it to you—when I'm gone, I mean—for being so kind to me. Charlotte would approve."

Juanita takes hold of my pale, blue-roped hands, presses them between her smaller brown ones.

"I, I mean, thank you, but—"

I squeeze her hand. "It's what I want."

She strokes my hair, starts to say that I'm getting so much stronger and shouldn't talk that way, but I interrupt, unable to stand the thought of her fingers encountering my greasy hair.

"Don't dear, it's not clean. They haven't let me have a shampoo in three days. Chills, they say. Really, they don't want to waste the shampoo."

Sometimes I grow so tired of apologizing for the body. I am no longer a pretty woman. Once—if she could have seen me then—I was something to look at, almost six feet tall with a straight back, long fingers, and thick, chestnut hair that curled up around my face in the heat. Some schoolteachers have to struggle to gain authority in the classroom, but my pupils seemed to have no concept of

mischief, or perhaps I frightened them, though I never once
raised my voice. At school, teaching French, I wore my hair
pinned up behind me, but at night, when I ushered at the
theater or played tennis in the park, I let it down. For sixty
years I washed my hair every day with a mild camomile
rinse. Juanita's hair has a blue sheen like a blackbird's wing,
each strand as thick and strong as upholstery thread. By
looking at a person's hair and fingernails, you can tell the
quality of their bones. I tell her I think of her as a daughter,
which is true some days, and she tilts her head and gives me
a funny look.

Juanita does not know that I am leaving her not just the
bracelet, but my entire fortune, which, though not enormous, is surely larger than anything she has ever known.
There is the inheritance from my grandfather, my savings
from over the years, and the money which will come when
my apartment and possessions are sold off. Left to the night
nurse. It would infuriate my mother, who believed in keeping things in the family, but there is no one I can think of as
more appropriate, Charlotte gone now, and the faces of all
the people I have known over the years dissolved into one
amorphous face—male or female, young or old, I cannot
tell. Perhaps this is what I am losing, for they do say that at
my age you are supposed to lose something—your teeth,
your bladder control, your mind. I have not lost any of these
things, but still somehow I seem to be losing track of the
people I have known. Often during the day I feel more like
an animal than a person, almost entirely self-possessed. I
know I must remember to call a lawyer, change my will,
but each day everything recedes except the drummings of
my body, the bulky shapes of the room, my voice register-
ing its automatic complaints to the stout day nurse.

And then at eleven each evening, Juanita. I watch the
black hands of my watch tense up as they near the proud,
symmetrical eleven. I cock my ear and learn to separate her
footsteps from the other noises in the hall. As if I were
eighteen, not over seventy. As if the world had shrunk to

the size of a room and all human presence had become contained in the clever body of this girl. At my age falling in love seems out of the question, but I exhibit all the silly symptoms, down to the palpitations of the heart. Or perhaps one can convince oneself of anything, given the need. Getting better frightens me, for I am not sure what I would use to plump out my hours, back home surrounded by my stacks of books and extensive collection of herbal teas. I manufacture complaints, a few each day.

"I'm dying," I tell the day nurse and doctors, and because I have plenty of money and really cannot get up, they have little choice but to contradict me firmly and let me stay.

Another night Juanita asks if I was ever married. I tell her yes, that it was nothing, and she wrinkles her nose.

"Nothing," she says. "How nothing?"

"He was a big newspaper reporter. He traveled a lot. We got divorced."

"You couldn't go with him traveling?"

I shake my head.

"Because of the children." She states it, leaves no room for argument.

"No children. We didn't get along. I had my job in the city."

"Why, then, did you marry him?"

I am afraid she considers me old and wise and is looking to me for answers. Sometimes when she thinks I am sleeping, she lets down her guard and sits staring off into space or drumming her hands aggressively on her white-stockinged knees. Then I doubt her happiness, with Robert James, with her husband the postman. She toys with the charms around her neck or stands in front of the mirror and sneers at herself. She looks years younger, then, a petulant child. Often she scrapes off her fingernail polish with her teeth and reapplies it with a small soft brush, spreading out her fingers and blowing hard until the lacquer dries.

"A mistake," I say, and Juanita runs her hand on the edge

of the dresser, checking for dust. She turns away from me to look out the window.

"And no children," she repeats.

I shake my head. "What? It's no tragedy. I wouldn't have wanted to bring a child into that marriage."

She shrugs, gazing at something outside, and I almost tell her how, in the smallest, most buried way, in a way I had almost forgotten, she is right—I would have been a fine mother, I have a way with children. They like me because I don't talk to them as if they were furry and stuffed. She might have come to visit me in the hospital, my daughter, grown now, tall and level-headed, brown-haired. She might have brought me books. From the beginning I would have taught her to read good literature, not junk like the pink and gold romances Juanita reads. You need to start early with an education, in the home. Juanita is not stupid—far from it—but she is happy reading trash, doesn't know any better. It's not her fault, not her mother's fault, but my daughter would have read the dark green, musty books I've saved from when I was a girl.

Down beneath the sheets, somewhere in my womb, I feel a pain—or hardly a pain, but a brief, forgotten cramping like that of my ancient periods, a fist expanding, a fist contracting.

"Aie!" I say, but when Juanita turns I tell her it is nothing, I am fine. I have learned that each part of my body starts to pain me more if I focus on it in my thoughts. As my thoughts leave my womb and travel up to my hands, my fingernails tingle and ache. As my thoughts leave my hands and climb to the roots of my hair, I feel each hair clinging to my dry skull like a determined weed. If I tug, even slightly, the hairs come loose like cobwebs in my hand.

I ask to see Juanita's wrist, to check it for size, and she perches next to me and places her arm on the covers like a gift. The bracelet will swim on her wrist; we will have to

61

get it altered. When I tell her so, she becomes gruff and hurried and says she is not accepting any bracelet. Right now, she says, she is going next door, late already. I should get some sleep.

"Yes," I agree, but I close my fingers around her wrist, and for a long moment we sit there in silence, she and I, her quick pulse beating against my thumb.

"When do you have your nights off this week?" I ask her, then, and release her.

"Tomorrow and Sunday," she says. I grab hold of her again.

"Tomorrow? Why didn't you tell me? Would you drop in and say hello to me? You know how much I miss you."

One day a few weeks ago, she left her purse in her locker, came in on her night off to pick it up. Now I pray for her forgetfulness. Leave your umbrella, I think. Leave your knitting, your muffler, your house keys. It is not easy to think of things important enough to make her come back.

"We're going to my mother's," she says. "We take the train. It's not a short ride."

"You could stop on the way. I'll give you money for a cab. It must be impossible on that crowded train with a little baby and all those people shoving."

"Oh no, he likes it—like a big rocking cradle," she says. "Remember, now, I'll be back on Thursday."

"Thursday night, almost Friday."

"But still Thursday."

"You don't know how the other nurse turns me over—as if I'm a big fat log. If you could just stop by on Wednes—"

"I told you, I go to my mother's."

"No, but on the way—"

She cuts me off, makes her voice artificially bright, the tone she must have learned in nursing school.

"So good—on Thursday night, I'll see you again. I'll miss you, too. You tell the doctor if the nurse turns you too hard, okay? They have girls who are plenty better than me at that. I'm not so good."

"I'll wait up for you," I tell her. "I won't be sleeping when you get here."

She laughs. "You sleeping? You're the famous night owl in this place."

She kisses my forehead and leaves.

It is true, most of the others sleep at night. It is why I have so much time with her; up and down the halls the others sleep hitched to respirators or with a leg in traction or breathing through one overworked lung. Juanita tends to these people, but it is a silent tending, and brief. They want nothing more, at night, than to be left alone. But I sleep during the day nurse's shift, or pretend to sleep, for I seem to need so little rest these days, as if the carpenters inside me cannot find it in themselves to stop tapping at my bones. Juanita used to read her romance novels at the nurse's station, but now she stays in my room and knits pale blue articles of clothing for Robert James. Hers is not a hard job, as nurses' jobs go, though the hours put a strain on her marriage; she has been working nights for the past few months, and her husband is not pleased.

"Why don't you work days?" I ask her Thursday night, and she says something about saving money on day care, and how when they are home for long periods together, they don't get along so well, the house too small. In her voice is something else, a tautness. Her fingers dart among the yarn, and she refuses to look up.

My revelation is swift and simple: Juanita stays working nights because of me.

Sometimes these things happen. Usually the timing is off, by a generation, by two or three. Usually nobody understands that anything could have been different. People get matched up with their next door neighbor, or their aunt's best friend's son, or the postman, and if they are not exactly overjoyed, they nonetheless have companionship and a body next to them at night. Most people assume, as they must, that this is enough, and treat their leftover yearnings—for the postman's sister, for the window cleaner, for a vague, luminous presence they have never seen but know must exist—as a kind of recurrent itch which will sink back into the skin for a while if only they can keep from scratching it.

But sometimes, through a hitch in the mechanism, people stumble upon each other, though the circumstances do not match at all. It happened with Charlotte and one of the guest teachers at the dance school. The Madame was old, gray, and pitiful in her leotard, moving like a remnant of herself, but Charlotte came home that day with glazed eyes and broke down crying at the dinner table, saying she thought she had to leave me. The Madame was married, ill, long past her prime. They had talked about dance for hours; she had massaged Charlotte's temples with her knotty hands. Charlotte didn't leave me, couldn't abandon me for a shadow, though we both knew the two of us were operating over a gap that would never fill itself in, despite all the years. She should have been my sister, Charlotte. I loved her enormously from the minute she ran up to me in the grocery store, but she and the dance teacher were something else altogether. Or perhaps it is simply that we place our foolish hopes in the things we know we cannot have.

Juanita brings me small gifts, mostly snapshots of her son and herself; she has discovered the self-timer on her camera and has taken roll upon roll of the two of them posed formally on the couch, staring the camera in the eye. Robert James wears something different in each photo, small changes—a baseball hat, blue booties, an embroidered bib. I can picture her dressing and undressing him like a doll. She does not bring me shots of her husband. We tack the photos to the bulletin board provided in every room, where most patients hang pictures of their families. The doctors don't give the board a second glance.

I teach her things—*bonsoir* and *à bientot*, which she rolls into the Spanish when she repeats after me. I teach her about what the French call *l'heure bleue*, the blue hour,

how it's not an hour but a second, really, a hinge—that
slivered moment when night is over, but day has not begun.
I want to show it to her out the window, point out the light
so feebly described by the color blue, but the streetlamps in
the parking lot stay on all night, and the sky is impossible
to read in such a glare.

65

Perhaps she is planning something. I can almost read it
into her smile, the way she starts to grin when she sees me,
then pulls the corners of her mouth down into something
more restrained. She asks me questions about my favorite
foods and how my apartment is decorated. If only she
would take me home. There, she might put the baby on the
bed with me and I might hold him, sing to him, change him
from one elaborate outfit to the next. She would not have to
work if she would rather stay at home, for money would
not be a problem. I could read to her from books, expand her
horizons, gossip with her about the neighbors she has already told me so much about. She is having trouble with
her houseplants, and I could show her how to clip them
back and wipe the leaves down with a sponge. I would
arbitrate disputes between Juanita and her husband, arrange
time for them to spend together, time for me to spend with
her alone, for each day she would shampoo my hair and give
me a long, hot bath.

It is not what it sounds like—I am beyond all that, would
expect it neither of Juanita nor myself. Not baths like I used
to take with Charlotte, when she sponged my back and
leaned over me, nibbling my skin like a silent, friendly fish,
our hands slick and smooth with soap. Juanita is a nurse,
and I, an old, sickly woman. She would bathe me with little
more than the dim recognition of missed opportunity—
what we might have been in another place and time. That
would be enough, her hands so capable and swift, and beads
of water catching on her hair. In such a place, bathed by
such hands, I would grow stronger every day until she could
leave the baby with me and go off shopping with her
friends.

I tell Juanita about the money I am leaving her. I cannot help it. She has come in frantic with worry—her sister has begun to talk to her about preschools, how only the private ones are any good, how Robert James will never go anywhere in life if he starts out wrong. There are waiting lists, her sister says. You can wait for years. Robert James, says Juanita, may have something wrong with him. He's too happy; he never cries, just sits and stares and drools. She thinks perhaps he has a learning disability. He'll be crushed in the public schools.

"I'm going to take care of you," I tell her, and she nods dismissively and says her husband wants to have another baby, afraid Robert James will grow up spoiled and lonely. He wants a sister for him, says Juanita, to teach him how to share.

"You won't need to worry about money," I tell her. "Anyway, I could babysit."

Now she is growing impatient; she glances at her watch. She will leave me any minute.

"Thank you, but I can't bring him to the hospital," she says.

"Juanita," I tell her, and something about my tone gets her to listen. "I have a good deal of money, and I don't need it. I'd like to help you out."

She takes a deep breath. "I can't do that."

"I want you to."

"Yes, but I can't."

"If you like," I say, trying to sound as if I just came up with the idea, "maybe I could come to your apartment some mornings and watch him. I'm feeling so much better lately."

She shakes her head and starts to walk away.

"Come here," I say. "Please."

My head has begun spinning. I know there must be a thousand ways to convince her, a thousand ways to get her to sit for a few minutes longer, to accept my help, but if I open my mouth I am sure to say something wrong, and then she will go away. I cannot be alone in the room, not at night after waiting all day. I must make her see that, or she will go stay with the others, who are sleeping and don't notice her sitting like an angel in the corner or bending over their charts. She turns around and stops several feet from my bed, her hands clasped behind her, her white shoes planted firmly on the ground. I pat on the cover for her to sit, and she backs away a few steps.

"What?" I say to her. "Did I do something? What did I do? Sit and talk to me for a minute."

She bows her head wearily, then perches next to me, her shoulders trembling, and begins to cry.

"Oh, little one," I say, but when I reach out, she slides away, inching further down the bed. "Shush now," I tell her, dropping my hand to the mattress. Exhaustion covers me like an extra blanket. "It'll be okay. He's a smart boy. I can tell from the pictures. He'll be fine."

She wears powdered blush on her cheeks, the tears weaving trails through the pink. I need to tell her how much she means to me, how miraculous it is, at this late date, to have stumbled upon her working here.

"I—" I begin, but she holds out her hand as if to wave my words away.

"Stop," she says, and there is such command in her voice that I obey.

And Juanita sits there, her small face turned away from me, and tells me she's been switched to days and not on this floor. That's the way it happens, she says, sometimes they just switch you, and she needs emergency room experience anyway, which is what she'll get, and they've offered her a small raise.

Did *they* switch you, I want to ask, or did you ask to be switched? Instead I tell her I don't know how I'll manage without her.

I should say *live,* not *manage,* but I do not.

She says she is sorry and hopes I will not give her the bracelet or anything else, because she wouldn't know what to do.

I tell her to please look at me when she talks, and she turns her face toward me, the lines set stubbornly, an unyielding face grown hard already in its shape. She swipes at her cheeks, smudging the blush and erasing the lines of tears. Poor Juanita, already growing old. I look at the face—such a stranger, so different from the face still glowing in my mind—and find that I, too, am crying. As the tears leave my eyes and begin to travel down my cheeks, her face relaxes and grows young again, swimming in liquid. She stands up when she sees me crying, puts a hand to her mouth and whispers, "Don't."

"I'm an old dying woman, and you have a need to be cruel to me," I hear myself say. It is the sort of self-pitying, overwrought statement I usually reserve for the day nurse, but I am clutching at straws, and what is more frightening is that suddenly it rings true: I am an old dying woman; she has a need to be cruel to me. The hammering in my body grows harder as if it has started sleeting inside my limbs, hailstones pelting into the marrow of my bones.

She leans over me—whoever she is, this night nurse, this stranger with an overdressed baby and postman husband—and whispers that she is sorry, she never meant to be cruel. She maneuvers me to a sitting position and holds me there, her cheek pressed up against my cheek.

"Stay, then, would you please?" I ask her, and she says no, she cannot stay, and lowers me down to the pillow. I try to sit, to say please again, but my head lolls like an overblown flower on a flimsy stem.

And then she is gone, and I am alone in the room with the string of cards clapping lightly in the breeze of her departure. For a moment I feel something smoldering in my bones like lit coals, a deep, indignant fury not so much against her as against all of them—the ones I have never met or couldn't have, the ones who spurned me, or loved me too slightly, or turned away from me before the disapproving face of the world. Against my sinking body, too, for its share in the abandonment, and my mind for somehow allowing a limp version of my old desire to live on. I lift my head, stronger suddenly, and look across the room to the bulletin board, still covered with pictures of Juanita and Robert James. Someone must take them down.

69

Then everything goes slack in my body, the hammering subsides, and I feel an airy sense of relief that I no longer have anything to look forward to—nights now the same as days, my peevish complaints free to circulate at will, my body free to air its indignities and shed its skin. I think of Charlotte, for it is she, finally, who deserves my thoughts, and of the bracelet and money I will still leave to Juanita if she will take them; she can use some help, and I can come up with no one else. I think of the old woman watching her husband's ashes flow. Such a small thing he became after a whole life—she could cup him in her palm.

I must have rung, for a nurse appears at my side, not Juanita, not the day nurse, but another woman altogether, her face as bland as hospital food, her warm consoling voice asking, "Mrs. Haven, what can I do for you?"

"The pictures, there," I whisper. "Could you take them down?"

I cannot seem to lift my head to watch her, but I know when she is through because her mouth appears above me saying she has put them in a pile on the nightstand. Someone will find them there and think, perhaps, that they are pictures of my daughter and grandson, though there is no resemblance between us. The nurse must have glanced down and recognized the face, because now she asks if she should return the photos to Juanita. No, I think. No, let them stay with me. So simple, photographs, so cooperative and flat—the beaming little night nurse and her son.

Out of the corner of my eye I see the hands of the new nurse tapping the edges of the photos on the nightstand, aligning them into a neat pile. Then she is gone from the room, the pictures with her, and I realize that I must have told her yes. In such ways we are stripped clean of everything we own. Even my own voice contradicts me, or perhaps I didn't answer and she took the photos anyway, thinking me asleep or close enough.

SCRAPS

On the map, Maine was a ragged, cut-up coastline, splintered as if a great clawed hand had swiped the land in passing, then moved on. It was a new map, still stiff as we spread it on the hood of Har's truck and squinted at it in the glare. Someone—I hadn't caught who—had thrust it at me as I walked down the aisle: a hand coming out, swiftly touching mine. Don't trip, I'd warned myself. It was a good gift, better than the bouquets of roses pressed into other graduates' arms, the blossoms already wilted in the heat. That morning the red of our disposable gowns had bled onto our arms and legs. Later, as we sat on the truck, Har had wet a tissue with saliva and rubbed at my leg. We had used the gowns to cushion our boxes in the back of the truck. As we drove north, it had begun to rain. The gowns were pink by the time we reached the ferry, almost white when at last we arrived at the house.

So full of his Aunt Elsie's things, that house—ribbons she had tied to doorknobs, postage stamps she had cut out from envelopes and placed like candy in glass dishes, animal skulls and rusty scraps of metal lined up like museum pieces on shelves. On the fridge door was a scrawled list addressed to guests: where to find sheets, how to light the stove, a number to call if the plumbing broke. Har and I held hands and crept through the house. She had not cleared it out, not cleaned it up. Empty glasses stood about; books were piled by every chair. The sea air circulated, cool. I wrapped a purple afghan around my shoulders. The bed in her room was unmade, a magazine open on the pillow.

"I feel like we're intruding," I whispered as we stood in the doorway. "She must use it all the time. Why do you think she told us we could stay?"

Har shrugged, hunched over as if he were afraid he would bang his head on the doorjamb. "She doesn't use it, only once in a while on weekends. Anyhow, it makes her happy to have us stay here."

And I decided it must have been his Aunt Elsie's hand at graduation, thrusting the rolled map like a baton in my path as I marched by.

At night there was motion—the waves outside, black and constant, Har's breath near my face, the salt air pushing through the window, damp as a pressing hand. It was not a honeymoon, for we were not married, not a vacation, because we did not work. We were to get our balance in that house, make plans before entering what everyone kept calling, much to my irritation, the real world. Elsie had given it to us for as long as we wanted because, Har said, she had taken a shine to me.

"A shine?" I'd said.

And he had laughed and said Elsie loved goofy old expressions like that.

Knowing him away from other people was such a different thing from knowing him in groups. In college he had organized expeditions to the bowling alley, the movies, concerts on the green—not bold about it, not loud, but somehow quietly effective; people gathered round. He had read two newspapers a day, gone running, turned in his papers weeks late, though he always managed to do well enough in school. He had gone from Harry to Har our senior year in one of those swift, odd decisions that seemed to emerge out of nowhere, Har pronounced like the first part of "hardly." At first I had been unable to decide if the switch was pretentious or funny. Finally I decided to view it as funny, for my own sake as much as his. Har wore dark red and forest green flannel shirts that set off his black hair—gifts from his mother and aunt.

At school we had only been alone in bed, every night for four months, my room or his, the delight of a body next to mine after so much time by myself. More than the delight, the astonishment—that I could give myself to this and be accepted, that my own small body made him gasp. At the end of each group outing we left together, saying, "We're tired," or "We're getting a cold," or "We've got work to do," as if it were as natural, as accurate, as saying "I." People accepted us so easily, began to blur our names together in one quick breath.

73

Everything surprised me: our laundry tumbling in one machine, how efficiently he sorted the clothes, turning my underwear and T-shirts right side out; the way he left pens covered with teeth marks and doodles of complex geometric shapes around my room; the way he wore the bristles of my toothbrush down on one end. In his desk I found a picture of a child in a bathing suit, ribs protruding, ears sticking out like shells. The kid was mugging for the camera with a huge, stretched smile. His elbows, his knees—everything about him looked sharp.

I had never seen a photograph of Elsie, but in early spring she appeared at school, stopped by to take us out to dinner on her way to an exhibit in New York. She was large, both tall and wide, and wore shades of brown and a heavy necklace of amber and silver beads. When I complimented it, she took it off and tried to give it to me. I must have looked truly panicked, saying, "No, no, I can't," because she finally took it back. An artist, Har said, and successful too. She made environmental sculptures, the kind that would burn up or sink back into the land—a bandaged tree leaning up against a giant stone, a funeral barge set on fire and sent down a river in flames.

I want to be this woman, I thought, then, picturing a black barge strewn with marigolds and moving slowly through dark water, the flowers blooming into flames. I wanted her height and magnitude, her bright voice—wanted to make beautiful things and let them float away. Her hands were large and open; her fingers could support thick silver rings. My own hands, twisting a dinner napkin into a tight spiral in my lap, looked more like tiny gnarled claws.

Aunt Elsie asked me questions: where I was from, what I was studying, what I thought about abortion. At first I tripped over my sentences, but as she filled and refilled my wine glass I became fluent and felt the roots of my hair tingle and my fingertips grow hot. I told her about the printmaking class I was taking, and she laughed and said yes, she had noticed the ink stains on my fingernails. I told her how none of the prints ever ended up looking anything like I'd planned. It must have been at that meal that Elsie took a shine to me; she nodded eagerly at everything I said. Har leaned next to me, brushing my arm with proud, feathery strokes. At dessert she offered us her summer house.

Alone there with him—how I woke the first morning and saw him lying there, his fist curled in sleep, the sheets twisted up around his ankles. Whose sheets? I had never seen those rose and purple stripes; the night before, perception dimmed by fatigue, I had assumed the sheets were white. We had taken the guest room, pushed two twin beds together and stretched on a double sheet. Har had wanted to use Elsie's large bed. "We can change the linens," he had said. "It's no problem." But it didn't feel right to me—the way we would have had to close her magazine, strip the bedding, seek sleep and each other in that room so full of someone else's belongings, her clothes still draped over a chair.

All night in the guest room we lay diagonally across the crack between the beds, Har's long legs dangling off the side. Several times I woke as he made noises and tossed. In the morning I watched him for a while; then I woke him with my hands. I expected, somehow, a clattering downstairs, eight or ten noisy friends making pancakes, someone singing or putting on a tape. We would all rent bikes and explore the island. Monday we would go back to school.

When, finally, we went downstairs, the kitchen was empty, bleached by the morning light. We found cans in the cupboard—chicken soup, baked beans, tomato paste, nothing for breakfast except a jar of applesauce. I parted the curtains and looked out to a clothesline and a pair of dilapidated lawn chairs, their dangling plastic strips loose in the wind.

"It looks like it'll be nice out. What do you want to do?"

He shrugged. "Check out the beach. See if the bikes in the basement work."

"I can't exactly picture her on a bike."

"Elsie?"

I nodded.

"She has a mountain bike; she rides it every day. But the ones downstairs are old junkers from when we all used to come up in the summers."

I didn't know who "we all" was. It could have been Har, his mother, stepfather, and brother Will. It could have been a larger, extended family I knew little about, a whole team of dark-haired, tall people steering their rusty bikes down to the sea. My own family was far away, in Pennsylvania. About them I knew a great deal, a lifelong catalogue of details, preferences, habits, and quirks. My relatives talked a lot; at family dinners it was a struggle to be heard. Har had been quiet when he had met my parents. They had been relieved that I had found a boyfriend, but worried to see us going off together, just like that. My mother had found a moment to remind me that I was still very young. Afterwards, Har had not questioned me about my family the way I had questioned him about his. I had wanted to know peoples' ages, their jobs, how they got along with each other, how he got along with each of them. I could see him growing impatient; soon I stopped. When I had asked him what he thought of my family as they walked away, he had said they were nice.

"Nice in what way?" I had pressed.

"You know, friendly. Nice." He had raised his hand in a wave, though they had not turned around.

And I couldn't tell anything, watching my family get into the car in their best clothes. Did nice mean boring? Did he see how sheltered their life was, how comfortable and moneyed, though his was not much different? Could he recite the clothing my family wore, the way they touched or did not touch each other in public? Could he describe their laughs the way I could with his family: his mother's hoarse and low, his younger brother's short and jagged, out of breath? Sometimes he remembered the most specific things: the names of local politicians, minor characters in old movies, words to songs that had played on the radio in junior high. Other times he didn't seem to notice much, or perhaps it was simply that his thoughts were somewhere else.

Har and I began to settle in. We drove to the one grocery store on the island and bought a week's worth of food. We dragged two bikes, thick and stubborn as old horses, up from the basement and oiled their chains. The smallest one was too big for me, but we lowered the seat, and I stretched my legs and managed to weave my way along the road. We had so much time, so much silence—no radio, no television, no chattering friends. I wanted to fill it up with talk, to start at the beginning with our earliest memories and systematically fill each other in.

I could do that. I had kept careful track, knew the layout of my first room, my favorite dress when I was five, the way my father would throw me up in the air, inspiring in me the purest, most wretched terror, then peer into my face to make sure I was having fun. I tried with Har, asked him to describe his elementary school, his first house, what he had liked to play at as a kid, but either he really didn't remember, or else he didn't want me to know. He would answer me shortly: the house was brick, the school was a normal school, he had played with the other kids.

I touched him then, the quickest way through. The

power of my own body dazzled me. It was like good food among strangers, or a lightning storm, or a deer in the road; it could fill up any lapse. In the silence I tried to think of things to say, then told myself I didn't need to try so hard, could get to know him slowly, over time. The four months at school seemed to compress into one or two; I couldn't think what we had accomplished. I began to buy the *Globe* and read the want ads. I thought I could be a teacher or social worker or perhaps some sort of environmentalist. Every ad was for manual labor or required an advanced degree. I read them aloud to Har on the beach: forklift operator, bus driver, clinical psychologist, high school principal.

"I'm going to be a pilot," he said, making a buzzing sound and nosediving his hand into the fold of my bent knee.

"No, but seriously, graduation money won't last forever," I said, latching on to his fingers. "Eventually we have to get jobs."

The "we" sounded awkward; immediately I wished I had made it clear how what I'd meant was each of us, not necessarily the two of us together. "I think," I said, "I might try to teach private school. The pay is lousy, but you don't need to be certified."

"We've spent fourteen dollars each in a week," said Har. "I don't know about you, but I can float along for a while at this rate."

We floated along. People on the island seemed to have lived there forever. You didn't need to have your car inspected, and the ones they drove were ancient and spotted with rust, their tin bellies low to the ground. I didn't understand what the islanders did all day, where they worked. Their houses were neat and quaint. They caulked their boats, picked berries by the side of the road, untangled elaborately snared kites from trees. Though some of them were rich and there for the summer, many seemed to be year-rounders, their eyes in a constant squint toward the mainland.

A neighbor brought us a lemon pie, her two small daugh-

78

ters at her side. Har stood chatting in the driveway, then lifted the older girl onto his shoulders and began galloping around the yard. I sat on the porch and watched. The neighbor eyed me: So young, I could imagine her thinking, and just the two of them. Har and the child circled, a totem pole come alive, the girl's hands buried in his hair. I thought about grabbing her sister and putting her on my shoulders—we could have a chicken fight—but the child stood gripping the hem of her mother's skirt and winced when I asked her name.

Rainy days I looked through Elsie's things: old photographs of stern people in bathing costumes like cut-off tights, a collection of broken eggshells—blue, brown, and speckled—in a shaggy nest, three tattered silk kimonos which I put on and paraded for Har. Do all these things make her happy, I wondered? All these used things, emptied of their original inhabitants: the nest and shells had housed birds, and the kimonos must have covered women in Japan. There was such care in the house, such attention to detail, but I couldn't decide if the place felt full of melancholy, like a husk, or full of life. Sometimes Har would join me, thumb through a pile of magazines. Often he read the paper, slept, or ran on the beach through the rain.

Once, as I lay awake in the middle of the night, he woke screaming, thrashing his arms in the air.

"Hey," I said, holding him down and trying to avoid his flailing arms. "What is it? You're only sleeping."

He was silent for a moment, breathing heavily. Then he blew out through his mouth. "God, that was wild—there was this huge—" He let out a weak groan.

"It's okay." I stroked his hair. "You're awake."

He nodded, took a deep breath. "Was I yelling?"

"A little. It's okay."

"Did I—I mean, what did I say?"

"You yelled, that's all."

"I used to say stuff in my sleep. I hate that."

"I've never heard you do that. What made you so scared?"

"It was, I don't know, just some stupid dream—I was in this sort of metal closet thing, and no one outside knew I could hear them, but they were all screaming that this steel—that this big steel plate or something was about to fall." He ran his hand over his face. "It doesn't matter, it was just a dream." His other hand, on the back of my neck, was trembling.

79

"You're shaking." I said.

I held him tighter, could feel him nod.

"It's a drag in some ways, huh?" I said. "I mean, being away from everything we've known for four years."

He shrugged and pulled me closer until our faces were touching in the dark.

I kissed his nose. "If it helps to talk—"

He pulled away and sat up, his voice cleared suddenly of sleep. "Listen, I don't need to shove everything out into the open all the time."

"Oh?"

"I mean it."

"No kidding."

"I'm serious, Naomi. I don't always needs to talk about *everything*."

"Oh right, and I do? There's a million things I never talk about. If you only knew."

"Like what?"

"Like if I told you, they wouldn't be the things I never talked about."

I started out trying to make my voice teasing, but it came out sounding cracked and close to tears.

He flopped back down, kissed the side of my neck. "Okay, I'm sorry. Forget it. We're both tired—I'm sorry I woke you up. Go back to sleep, okay?"

"I wasn't sleeping."

I was silent for a moment, then my voice came out clear in the dark. "Do I really do that, do you think?"

"Don't sound so worried. I'm not saying it's a fault. I'm just saying it's the way you are, and it's kind of—exhausting sometimes, is all. But it's no big deal. Go back to sleep."

For a moment I wanted to tell him it was because I cared about him, but then I realized that perhaps it was only because I cared about myself. I needed to talk, all the time, about everything; if I didn't talk, my life might lose sight of itself and disappear, the way people with no baby pictures couldn't conceive of ever having been so small. I needed voices around me, not just his, but many voices. I needed a job where I was expected at a certain hour, where a great many things piled up on my desk and I finished the day reeling and tumbled into sleep. I was beginning to think I didn't like islands—only one store to go to, one overpriced gas station. I hadn't spoken to anyone but the neighbor and Har in days.

I swung my knees over the side of the bed. He caught me gently by the wrist.

"Where're you going?"

I would go to Elsie's room to sleep, wear somebody else's silk kimono to bed. I tried to tell him, but as I stood up, the words caught, and I gestured dumbly in the dark.

"To the bathroom?" he said, and I answered no.

"Don't go away," he said, stroking the hairs on my arm in the wrong direction so that I shivered. "Don't go, okay? Stay with me right here."

And then he was pulling me down with his soft, insistent hands, and I was falling back beside him on the bed, breathing in his smell.

I could go on like this, I realized, for years. I pressed against him and decided I should leave within a week, before I had forgotten how to live alone.

In the morning, Har and I awoke to the smell of coffee. Downstairs we found Elsie with bags of food from the mainland, a red and black scarf tied around her head.

"Breakfast?" she asked and leaned to kiss us.

"Look at you two—you look terrific," she said. "All that

fresh air and romance, right? How long have you been here? Around ten days?"

Har nodded.

"Eleven days today," I said.

"I hope you don't mind my just showing up. I tried to call Gracie next door so she could warn you, but it was busy for so long—finally I gave up. Poor thing, all her friends are on the mainland. She goes a little nuts out here."

I wondered if Gracie was the one with the pie.

"Elsie," said Har, "it's your house."

She looked around, curious, as if she'd never been there before, and picked up a salt shaker shaped like a cactus. "So much junk—can you believe it? Someday I've got to have a tag sale and get rid of all this stuff. Every piece of garbage I don't want on the mainland I bring out here."

But her voice was proud. She looked at me, deep into my eyes, a searching look. Nobody, I realized, had looked at me like that in a while. I looked away. Har had begun unloading groceries on the counter.

"How are you, Naomi?" his aunt said.

I smiled thinly. "Fine."

"You're the first girl Har has ever brought out here. Isn't that right, Harry?"

I didn't turn around in time to see how Har responded, but he must have done something funny because Elsie laughed and swatted the side of his head.

That night we ate lobsters and clams, pasta salad, grilled tomatoes, chocolate and strawberries, with glass after glass of red wine. Elsie and Har sang songs, their dark eyes shining; I had forgotten how merry he could be, how boisterous in groups. The two of them picked up lobster claws and waved them to the music. Har dangled an antennae from his mouth like a cigarette.

"Remember this one?" Elsie would ask me, beginning to sing. "Or this one?"

But I didn't know these children's songs full of ducks and frogs and nonsense words.

"I'll listen," I said. "I can't carry a tune."

Already I was dizzy from the wine. Har had drunk a few glasses and seemed to be growing tired, but Elsie kept coming up with song after song. Har would listen to the first bar, then seem, despite himself, compelled to join in. She looked good for her age, his aunt, robust and healthy, her face lit with nostalgia, three wooden bracelets clanking on her wrist. Each time a song ended she thought of another, then another. I remembered the story of the red shoes—the girl who couldn't stop dancing, who danced until she dropped.

"Remember this one?" said Elsie, singing: "John Jacob Jingleheimer Smith, his name is my name too!"

She waited a second, looked at Har, but he shook his head and coughed.

"I'm beat, Aunt Elsie. You beat me. My voice is dying."

He locked eyes with me for an instant as if to say *help me out here*, leaned over the kitchen table, and grabbed my hand. "Bedtime?"

"Now?" said Elsie, and I thought I heard an edge of panic in her voice. It was dark out and must have been quite late. The kitchen counters and table were strewn with dirty dishes. I, too, could feel exhaustion tugging at my limbs. For the first time since graduation, I felt the pleasure, the sense of privacy and privilege, of knowing I could go off with Har to another room, a shut door. It only worked when there were other people in the house. I was grateful, then, in my own selfish way, that she had come.

"You go ahead, lazybones," said Elsie to Har. "Naomi and I are going for a walk. Will you do that, Naomi?" Underneath its gaiety, her voice was pleading. I looked at Har.

"Shouldn't we clean up a little?"

"Oh that can wait until tomorrow," his aunt said. "Come."

This time it was a command, and I did not argue. Har kissed us both goodnight and disappeared down the hall.

When the screen door slammed and the lights of the

kitchen fell away, we became two silent, unsteady women groping our way toward the beach.

"Give me your hand," said Elsie after I tripped and let out a small yelp. I extended it in the dark, and she took hold. Her hand was larger than mine, cool.

"I used to be able to walk this blind," she said. "Keep your arm in close—the beach roses have thorns. Oh dear, I don't come up here enough anymore."

On the beach it was easier to see, the moon out from behind a cloud and a lighthouse on a nearby jetty sending out its beam. Elsie bent and picked up a piece of driftwood, ran her hands over its surface, then tossed it to the sand.

"It's like a sculpture I did once," she said. "The shape."

"What's your stuff look like?" I asked, remembering my own clear image of the barge, which I was sure now must have been inaccurate, the colors or proportions wrong. Har had given me so little information. Why had I pictured a wide, slow river at night and seen marigolds on the barge? Why did Elsie *burn* her sculpture anyway? Suddenly it seemed sort of pitiful to me, a stagey bit of melodrama. If the barge had been mine, I would have left it on some beach to be slowly nibbled at by water, sand, and salt.

"Har tried to describe some of your pieces once," I said, "but I couldn't quite see."

She laughed, a short, barking laugh. "Nothing to see, after a while. They're biodegradable. Like that piece of wood."

"Are they big?"

"Bigger than a bread box. How would you like to go for a swim?"

"In there? It's so cold, even during the day."

"Not cold. Refreshing. This is Maine, Naomi. Won't you come in?"

I shook my head, and she began to strip. I looked away as her clothes dropped in a pile to the beach, then watched her walk resolutely to the water, her hair unpinned and falling heavy down her back. When she got to the edge she let out a groan, then pushed forward and plunged herself into the sea.

"It's lovely. Cold, but lovely!" she called as she came up from under and stood waist-deep in the water. I slipped off my sandals and walked to the edge. The water lapped around my ankles, so cold my arches cramped. I could see Elsie's head and arms to my left; she had begun to swim slowly along the shore. She turned and made her way back until she was in front of me, then stood. The water glinted, streaming down her breasts.

"Sing to me, Naomi, would you?" she called.

I tried to think of a song. She knew I didn't know any; I had said so at dinner. I searched my brain but could only come up with "My Country 'Tis of Thee."

"I really can't follow a tune," I called back. "You're better off just listening to the waves."

"Then come in! It's perfect."

"It's freezing. My feet are about to fall off."

"Then sing to me." Her voice was insistent, almost nagging. The wine had left me feeling worn out and limp, but perhaps it was still sending bubbles through Elsie's veins.

"What do you want me to sing?"

For a moment she was silent. Then she said something I couldn't make out. I stepped slightly deeper.

"What? I can't hear."

"I said, you must know 'Happy Birthday.'"

I winced. "Oh, no—it's not—why didn't you tell us?"

I backed up onto the beach, took a deep breath and began to sing, facing toward her, my voice thin and quavery as a child's or old woman's. I wasn't sure, couldn't hear myself well enough, but I assumed it was badly off-key. When I finished, Elsie came and stood next to me, naked and shivering, so tall beside me. She wrung the water from her hair.

"Thank you."

"If we had known—"

"Oh no, it wasn't today. It was two weeks ago. My gallery

threw me a huge party. I'm just being spoiled, just wanted
to hear it on the beach. Thanks, Naomi."

She stepped back a few steps, twirled around. "How do I
look, do you think, for fifty-two?"

I looked at her wide hips, her large, low-slung breasts, a
silver necklace disappearing between them. I had never
been able to stand naked before other people. Even with
Har, I groped for my panties the minute I got out of bed. I
felt so small beside Elsie, I was afraid I would vanish in the
sand.

85

"You look terrific."

"Thanks. What else are you supposed to say? But thank
you, because I think you mean it. You're a lovely girl."

I grimaced.

"Don't give me that look," she said. "You *are.*"

She walked up the sand to where her clothes lay in a heap
and began to dry herself off with her sweatshirt, peering
down at her legs.

"It's true, I don't look so bad, do I?" She sniffed. "For
whatever that's worth. Do you think you'll stay with him?
He's a good person, Harold. He has a very good heart. I've
watched him grow up—he was a gentle baby. Do you love
him? I can tell you at least like each other quite a bit."

"I don't know," I said slowly, standing near her. "It
hasn't been very long. I guess we don't know each other
very well. He's—he's hard to get to know, or maybe it's
just me."

She pulled on her pants and T-shirt, flung the wet sweatshirt around her neck. How relieved I was to see her dressed
again—perhaps her wine was wearing off. She turned to
face me, put her hands on my shoulders. What, I wondered,
does she want from me? I could smell wine and chocolate
on her breath.

"Everyone," she said, "is hard to get to know. I realize
I'm just somebody's old aunt, but can I give you some advice? Young people expect too much. Companionship, a

body, sweetie—these are things of value. Don't expect too much. Har wouldn't hurt a flea. Oh—"

She shuddered. "I sound like I'm telling you to settle for the first Joe who comes along, don't I? It's just that—in the funniest way you remind me of myself at your age. Not that we're alike, just that—oh I don't know . . . maybe all I mean is you must try to be a little flexible—"

She lifted her arms from my shoulders and flopped them about in the air. "You'll settle in your ways so quickly. It gets harder and harder as you grow old."

And I wanted to ask her why she didn't have someone—a woman, an artist, as dynamic, as comfortable in her body as she. But then I thought of her room, her house, so clearly the house of a single person, the objects lined up like talismen—not one collection but so many you hardly knew where to begin drawing categories. It had felt, that first day as Har and I toured the rooms, as if we were stepping on the folds of someone's brain.

"You're shivering," I said, and as she nodded I saw myself at fifty-two. I would have grown more and more set in my ways, more and more alone, until people respected my rituals, my aloneness as if I were encased under a glass bell like the automated dancer on my old music box.

And then I had pitched my body forward and was holding her, this large woman, Har's Aunt Elsie, her tangled hair and wet sweatshirt damp against my face. It was as if by warming her, I could prevent my own future trembling, as if by getting so close that I could not see her, I could keep us both on the narrow rim of possibility where I was hovering still.

We stood that way for a long time. She was silent and smelled of the sea. I thought of my mother, who was a much slighter woman, of Har, who would wake in the night and reach for me with a desperateness I never saw in daylight. Once in biology class I saw a film about monkeys who were nursed by metal mothers and comforted with scraps of flannel cloth. They could not live that way, those monkeys, could not grow up without the comforts of the flesh. At the end of the film they cowered thin and quivering under a jungle gym, as if waiting out an earthquake or a war.

Elsie let go of me, turned toward the house. She put out her hand; she would lead me back. I could tell from her grip how badly she needed to believe in me and Har—how badly she needed me to believe. She had said she could tell that Har and I liked each other quite a bit, but I wasn't even sure, just now, how true that was. I could see how Elsie viewed the two of us—how young we seemed, how leaning into love. It didn't matter that she was an artist. Like anyone else, she would see what she wanted to see.

Upstairs, Elsie would fall asleep in a room sacred with her possessions, cradle a pillow against herself; I knew— I had done it myself for years. I would fall asleep curled against someone else, so lucky for a moment, but as soon as my eyes shut, I would leave him. Sleeping, he would have left me long ago.

Or perhaps he would be dreaming of me, just when it seemed he was farthest away. And perhaps I was wrong about Elsie—maybe she was happy by herself or had hidden a lover in the closet or left one in the city. Maybe she couldn't care less about what happened between me and Har. What did I know about my boyfriend's aunt—how she slept, how she viewed the objects on her shelves? What did I know about my boyfriend? Such gall, such cockeyed innocence for me to have agreed to come out here in the first place. I had not thought twice.

What I did know—intimately, accurately, over time— was the rhythm of my own steps, the weight of my own bones, my wrist caught between Elsie's fingers as she led me back. I wanted to pull free and stop there in the path, to lie on the sand which would mold itself more closely than another body to my shape.

How wrong, how ungrateful, I knew, to be so difficult. But then it was late at night, and I had drunk too much wine, and the point was that I wouldn't stop, but let her lead me. And there—up the stairs, through a door—he'd be, not supple like sand, but almost. Har, for I was (how grown, how lucky, if I could only stop thinking) a woman with a lover in a house on the edge of the sea.

THE BOY
WHO FELL
FORTY FEET

The girl he loved was shy and quick and the smallest in the class, and usually she said nothing, but one day she opened her mouth and roared, and when the teacher—it was French class—asked her what she was doing, she said, in French, I am a lion, and he wanted to smell her breath and put his hand against the rumblings in her throat.

The boy he loved was in the class above and came from a faraway Arab country and was called Rachid. When the others wore navy blue, Rachid wore red, and when the others cut their hair short, he let his curl well below his ears, and when the rest of the boys joined in a huddle before soccer games, wrapped their arms around each other's shoulders and cried out, the Arab boy stood by himself and closed his eyes, and with him they always won.

The boy didn't know how anyone could move that fast, Rachid a churning tangle on the field. He didn't know how anyone could hug that close to the ball or arc it so smoothly toward the net. In the end it didn't matter, because a dark, thick happiness almost choked him at the moment time ran out and he knew that nothing could change the score, and he breathed the clinging, sour smell of grass and mud and leapt with the other boys. Then, in the locker room comparing bruises, they sang together, school songs or something vaguely bawdy, or the national anthem tinged with sarcasm. Only a few things equaled this for the boy— having his feet measured for new shoes, bending a piece of orange peel until a fine spray shot up, falling asleep in the car—when they had a car—and the smell of gasoline. There were so many things to think about, so many different ways, he thought, to get it off his mind. That was what his aunt said to his mother: "Go to a movie, get a haircut, anything to get it off your mind." And the boy pictured his mother's mind like a breakfast tray, bent in the middle from overuse.

At home, alone in his room, he would start at the top of his head and run his hands down over his face, over his narrow chest, down to his knees and feet, and then sometimes he would lie on the floor and try to force his legs back behind his neck like the Pretzel Man. He had plenty of time for this lately and was sure that eventually he would succeed.

His mother had a job to bring home money, but also, she said, because going to work as a secretary forced her to think a little about things like lipstick, stockings, and cutting her hair. She had a microwave, so fast and simple, and bitter pine oil for baths so hot they burned—the only remedy for muscle ache and city grime. Often at night they would get ready for bed at the same time, and then the boy's mother would settle down in her room to watch an old romance or western on TV. Later the boy would wake to voices and wonder who was talking in their house.

At school the teachers saw him as nicer and more inclined to help than he really was, and often they asked him to open the windows, shut the blinds, or erase the blackboard, which he did with a tight, obliging smile on his face and with his mind on the lion girl or Arab boy or other things. Every once in a while, knowing his situation, his teachers tried to talk to him outside of class, but his eyes would wander to the door or window, and he would answer, "I'm fine, she's fine, he's fine," as if conjugating a verb. His mother left him notes: "Hi. Back at nine. Do your homework and there is a nature special on TV at eight if you want." Or, "Please do *not* answer the phone because it could be the insurance people." She brought him pens from work now and then, and when she got home from the hospital she came in to say goodnight and express her thanks that he was such a grown-up kid and bearing up so well under the pressure, because any added trouble and she would crack, she said, although he could not imagine it.

When she brought him with her, which was not often, he bought candy in the gift shop and scuffed his shoes across the glossy floors. One day a nurse gave him a rubber surgeon's glove, which he blew up like a cow's udder, and a woman in a wheelchair waved him down in the hall and asked for the story of Bessie the Cow. The boy said he didn't know it; he grew shy, yet stood there frozen with the inflated glove.

What he wanted very badly was the facts—was it her legs or an invisible something else? The woman smiled, and her head didn't wobble. She asked his name, and her words didn't blur together at each end. He wanted to yank the afghan from her lap and peer below, but there was his mother, apologizing to the woman, chiding her son for not reading his comic book on the bench. That was why kids could only come visit now and then, she said. The staff was afraid they would catch things or make noise.

Sometimes the boy wrapped himself around his pillow at night, and other times he played word games and chanted to himself. "My old man is kicking the bucket, my papa is passing away, my dad will soon be dead."

I am the only one in my school like that, he thought, although he couldn't be sure, and often he imagined that he lived alone, for it was almost true, and that he had always lived alone. One day they read about the Mayan Indians who were waiting for the end of the world, and he realized that his life had grown calm and stretched like the insides of a balloon, and that since he had turned eight two years ago and his body had begun to wake him up at night and his father's body had begun to nibble on itself from the inside out—since then, he had been quietly waiting for everything to end and begin.

Coming out of school, he spied on them: the girl, who set off alone, wearing a plaid raincoat even on the sunniest of days; Rachid, who leaned against the brick wall waiting for his brothers and sisters and broke into that language when they appeared, noisy as a clattering subway car, and left without looking back. His house, thought the boy, was probably so full of people you couldn't help bumping into them everywhere you went, and probably all the children slept in one wide bed. The lion girl had an older brother at the high school—she had said it once in class—and if she ate too much sugar something happened to her blood so that she grew pale and brought her hands to her face, her face to her knees. He knew everything she wore, the colors of her notebooks, and her locker number: S417. He had nearly mastered the art of looking at her sideways or through lowered lashes, but when she caught him he wished he had never begun, and a taste like the tip of his pencil filled his mouth.

His father said the drugs they gave him made him feel all soft and changed the way his skin felt, so that he wondered if he were growing fuzz like a peach. Once he had been the manager of a large sporting goods store, and often now when he couldn't sleep, he told his son, he counted inventory in his head. The boy pictured the rows of football jerseys and tennis rackets, the hockey pads to protect the athletes from each other, the smooth white Chapsticks to protect them from the sun and wind.

"See how he's glad to see you," his mother said when her husband closed his eyes. "He's having a real good day."

"I got to go to the bathroom," whispered the boy.

"Just tell him good-bye."

"I *got* to go," he said, and his mother took him out.

Most afternoons he went home to read her daily note and make sure nothing had changed, then put on the dirty yellow baseball cap they wouldn't let him wear in school, hunched up his shoulders, and went to roam or prowl. It was his mother who called it roaming, "senseless roaming," but the boy preferred the word *prowl*, which was what animals did, because it made him think of secrecy and grace and some kind of final catch. He knew his neighborhood at least as well as the postman and probably, he thought, as well as the bums and maybe as well as the stray dogs, who could see around corners before they got there.

One afternoon in May, while his mother was at work, the boy perched on a mailbox like a gargoyle, examining the bottom of his sneaker. He was wearing it out in a funny way, he saw, so that the sole on the inside of the foot was thinner than the rest.

Do something, he said to himself, so he jumped down from the mailbox, walked into an alley, and kicked a trash can, then bashed at it again until the front of his foot tingled and he had made a small dent.

Something else, he told himself. Walk down by the river, where there are rats.

So he walked past the Chinese grocery with its squares of tofu plunged like soap in a tub outside, past the curb where he had seen a man vomit into his hands, past the basketball court where his father had once played with him in the hot sun, and the boy had not known whether to be happy and pleased with the new orange ball, the afternoon devoted to sports, or embarrassed at the slight paunch his father had (and then lost) and the way he yelled too loudly and told the boys on the other court that their ball could use some air.

Someday, thought the boy now, shoving his hands into his pockets, there'll be no more court and no more basketball and all those boys will be gone, and he tried to strip the city to what had once been there, which must have been air and a skinny dog or two and a lot of dirt.

When he saw a penny on a manhole cover, he picked it up, and when he passed a woman making snow cones, he stopped to watch, and when he saw scaffolding and men in hard hats and flannel shirts, he snuck around back where they were no longer working and began to climb. On the first level he found an empty paper bag left from someone's lunch, and on the second level he found a pile of screws and pocketed a few. Climbing reminded him of his body, of pulling himself up by his arms, and he wrapped his hands around the sun-warmed metal pipes and felt his jeans stretching with his legs. He passed the windows like a shadow and assessed the height as he reached the fifth level, then the sixth level, then the top. At the top, he lay down on the rough wooden boards and looked down through the cracks.

Below, he could picture them standing in a circle—his mother, his father, the Arab boy, the lion girl. His father was draped between his mother and Rachid, the girl was off by herself a little—four faces tipped toward him like different sized planets, only narrowed by the crack. They were there to look up at him, after him. They were there to marvel at the distance. The boy looked down again and saw a taxi and a moving van, a man with a shopping cart, one kid pinning another against a wall. He put his head down on the board to smell the girl and smelled instead the pitchy scent of wood. He pressed down on the platform and felt his heart crowd against the sharpness of his ribs.

At the end of the alley was the river, and next to the river was the building site where he often looked for rats, and at the edge of the site, stretching its neck over a makeshift sidewalk and a pit, was a yellow crane. A woman was walking that day along the sidewalk. It had never happened before and probably would never happen again, but as the crane leaned forward to hoist its load of metal rods, it lost its balance and tumbled forward like a thirty-five-ton bird.

For a moment, movement: the pavement cracking, weight shifting as the crane's base pushed the plywood barrier halfway down the pit's slanted side. A crumbling of earth. Then a creaking sound, a groan of metal against wood, and the tipped base came to rest precariously against the displaced plywood barrier and settled, overgrown and awkward, across the fallen woman's lap.

From the scaffolding the boy saw the glint of yellow and

heard the scraping noise, and then he heard sirens and began to scramble down. By the time he had run the length of the alley to the site, the woman had opened her eyes to a crushing weight on her legs, pushing the sense out of her, knocking her silly, so much pain she felt she had been lifted to another world.

"There's a lady down there," said a teenager to the boy, and they stood with the others at the edge of the roped-off area. Some people bit their nails, and others prayed, for they had already brought in a priest.

Maybe, thought the boy, they needed someone small and careful to bring her things, because the police and medics had succeeded in communicating with the woman, and she had tugged twice on the rope they had lowered to say, "No, I can't move my legs," and once to say, "Yes, I'm all right," and once more to say, "Yes, a priest."

"They know she's alive but they don't know how to move the crane," said the teenager to the boy, and they peered at the machine, which was tipped against the side of the pit at a crazy angle, as if waiting to slide further down the hole. "Move it wrong and she's a goner, huh?"

The boy nodded and ducked off, tunneling his way through the crowd to the edge of the roped-off area, stretching his neck to see.

I'm small enough, he thought. I could fit down there no problem and help her out, but when he inched toward the edge of the pit, a policeman pushed him back as if he were a pesky dog and told him to get on home.

The boy made his face distant as if he hadn't heard, but the cop waved a hand before his face.

"Yoo-hoo mister, I'm talking to you! No kids on the premises. Scram, or I'll have to turn you in."

So the boy left the lady and the crane and went back to the scaffolding, but they were working where he'd been. He went down another alley closer to home and kicked at an empty metal garbage can lying on its side until it rolled. Then he leapt on top of it, lost his balance, fell, and got up

95

to leap again, balancing and falling his way down the alley like a half-broken machine until his jeans and shirt were streaked with grease and dirt, and bruises painted his cheeks and arms. When he got to the end of the alley, he turned the other way and started back. This time he whispered "All right! All right!" and pressed his fingers to his palms, knowing he'd caught the rhythm of the thing.

It was a question of moving your feet at the same speed as the can, or no, moving them a tiny bit more slowly because the feet pushed the can forward and made it go. It was a question of leaning back just enough to avoid going over the front edge, but not so much that you got left behind. Timing and balance, he thought, balance and timing, and he remembered the athletes who came to his father's store, the careful way they talked about their sports. He found he could go ten, twelve, twenty feet at a time, arms flailing in crooked circles, teeth clenched. He was the only one in the alley, and he could hear nothing but the hollow sound of the can, the pounding of his feet, the ragged intake of his own breath. He could feel nothing but his own body until the pressure of a hand wrenched him from the moving garbage can, landing him so hard on his left ankle that he fell forward to his knees.

"You always screw around with other people's property?" said a voice as the boy stumbled up, and the hand came down on his shoulder to shake him hard. The boy winced at the pain in his ankle and shut his eyes the way he used to when his mother yelled at him. He heard: "Where you from? You think this city is a goddamn playground? You've got nothing better to do with your time?"

Then the voice stopped talking, and the boy opened his eyes to find it belonged to a bulky man in a red T-shirt with a ratty little girl at his side.

"You got nothing to say for yourself?" said the man.

"My father died," said the boy, and the words hovered in the alley like suspended bells, so clear he knew they must be true.

"Aw shit," said the man, reaching out to touch the girl's head. "Today?" he asked, and the boy nodded and watched his sneakers, which were coated with a fine layer of dirt.

"Aw shit," said the man. "You better get on home. You got a mother at home?"

The boy opened his mouth to say no, to tell the man he lived alone, that he had always lived alone, but instead he found himself nodding, and the man said, "Okay, good," and rubbed the girl's neck. "You better get on home," he repeated, so the boy said "yeah" and turned to go.

On the way back, he mumbled it: "My father died, my father died," and nobody noticed because it was the city. Limping from his twisted ankle, exaggerating how much it hurt, he tried to picture his father with a pain like this, with a worse pain—so hot it burned you up until you turned white, then gray, then disappeared. Once, the boy had not known about hospital smells or how beds went up and down like dentists' chairs or the way people could eat through rubber tubes. He had not known the elastic possibility of change, and then one day he had come home to find the world on a whole new axis, everything slightly tilted, like a bike on crooked training wheels.

My father, he thought, was a goddamn honest man. His mother had said it on the phone to her sister: "How could I *not* tell him what the doctor said? You got to talk straight to him. He's such a goddamn honest man." His father was tall, a jokester, with hair in his nostrils and on his back and a way of tossing his head like a horse. That's all I know, thought the boy—all I remember, because the rest came from after. He sat down on a stoop a block from his house and lowered his head to his knees.

You dummy, he said to himself. You dumb-head, get up, and he tried to think of something he might like to do, but he was so tired, as if someone had drained away his blood. He tried to think of things he liked, but his mind went blank, so he thought of things he disliked and remembered the time his father had smacked him on the side of the head because he had stuck a pen into the pilot light of the stove. It had not been a gentle slap, meant to teach. It had wrenched the boy's neck and left a red mark on his face, and later he had snuck out and poked tiny holes with the pen in the seat of his father's car.

"Shit shit shit," whispered the boy into his hands, because he missed his father so much he couldn't move.

When he got home his mother was not there, and he pulled down his shade, crept into bed, and held himself. Later she came to the door, peered into his room, and said, "Asleep already? It's only nine," and he turned to display his cuts and bruises in a swatch of light. His mother wore an orange sweater and lavender skirt—she wore only the brightest colors—and her shoulders drooped. When she looked at him, she sighed and said, "Oh no, not a fight," and turned on the light by his bed.

"Was it a fight?" she said, unbuttoning his pajama top to see where he was hurt, and he shook his head dumbly, and then, for the first time in front of his mother in at least a year, he began to cry.

"It *was*. Those bastard kids," she said, lowering herself to perch on the edge of his bed. "Those little bastard city kids. We have to get you into a different school."

She put out her hand to pat the blanket covering him and breathed in, as if gathering her energy.

"Tell me about it," she said.

So he told her how he had been down by the river, and there was this big crane—you know, over where they're building that apartment building—and he had been walking along looking for rats, and suddenly the earth had fallen out from under him.

"No!" said his mother. "I heard about that! They were talking about that at the hospital, all the nurses."

"Yeah, well I fell twenty, maybe thirty or forty feet," he told her, and she moved closer to him and took his hand.

"It's crazy. Thank God you weren't badly hurt. They should have taken you to the hospital."

"I know," said the boy, wiping his face on the cuff of his pajama top. "Except nobody saw me, and there was this lady buried by the crane. They had this ladder over on the other side, and I just sort of climbed out alone."

"Really?" said his mother. "Really, did you do that? All alone?"

"Yes," he said, and he knew she didn't believe a word of it. She was holding his hand, and he was leaning toward her, and then she was saying something, but he couldn't make out the words.

"What?" he asked, but she shook her head.

"He liked your drawing, I think," said his mother, and for a minute he couldn't remember which drawing, but then he knew it was the one in india ink, the face of someone he had invented, a girl.

"Come here," said his mother, and for the first time in a long time she held him as if he were a young child, and he breathed the warm air against her chest until she pulled away, too soon, and said she was tired and would get ready for bed.

"It'll be okay," she said as she turned to go, and he blocked his ears with his fingers and burrowed down under the quilt, but he could sense his mother hovering in the room, so after a minute he surfaced and lowered his hands.

"I'm sorry," she said from the doorway, half in, half out. "I'm so sorry about all of this," and her voice sagged, then rose again. "Rest is important, isn't it? Sleep well, pumpkin, okay?"

What she didn't know was that he couldn't fall asleep, not for the first hour after she left, not for the second hour, not for what seemed like the entire night. He drummed his fingers against the wall to the beat of songs. He took his flashlight from the milk crate by his bed and inspected the corners of the room. He got up to run his fingers over the books and cars on his shelf, then climbed back in with the flashlight and a mystery, but the print was small and strained his eyes. I should count, he told himself, so he turned off the light and thought of thirty pairs of skis, eighty baseball bats, but the numbers stretched before him to infinity and made him more awake. His leg ached from where he had fallen, and he pressed on the tender spot until his hand grew stiff.

My mother is sleeping, he thought, and he knew just how she looked, flat on her stomach in her blue flannel nightgown under the plaid comforter, her head buried under her arms. Next to her bed, he knew, was the lamp shaped like a soldier holding a torch, and under the bed were her pink quilted slippers and some wadded Kleenex and some dust and maybe a gum wrapper, and on her night table were her gold rings and the clock they had gotten free from the bank, the alarm set to 6:15. And my mother is breathing, he thought, first shallow breaths and then deeper breaths, and her mouth is slack and her fingers are limp, and my mother is sleeping.

My father, he thought—

But they had put his father in a plain old hospital room, nothing special about it, and the boy didn't know how to go on.

THE
EXPERIMENTAL
FOREST

When I was a child, my parents saved and saved, then bought us a piece of land in the middle of the woods. The land was a steal, cheaper than anything around, since it bordered on a forest where the trees had been injected with viruses and tagged with metal plaques. On their plot of troubled land, my family built a one-story, three-bedroom, hunched-over wooden house. In the spring, we saw the leaves appear on the poplar trees like green silver dollars. In the fall, we watched them drop like yellow silver dollars to the ground.

When we first moved in the trees were not much bigger than the house, but as the years passed and my brother Warren and I grew our mild inches, the poplars shot up with all the appearance of runaway good health until I had to crane my neck to see the tops. When the wind blew, I could see the poplars bent like bows, curved to the breaking point. Then, just in time, the wind would turn, and the groaning trees would straighten out. The year I turned fourteen, half the poplars began to drop yellow leaves in midsummer, and I looked out to see government men putting small red dots on the trunks of the sick trees.

"This is crazy," I told my parents. "Why don't they cure them now?" But they had been forewarned and could only sigh.

"A bargain is a bargain," said my father. The men did not cut down the trees. All around us the poplars grew brittle and lost their leaves. Walking up the driveway from the bus stop, I took death tolls: three, nine, twelve. Sometimes I scanned for tree men, and then, when I was sure the path was clear, I took my penknife and scraped off the circles of paint, just to give them something to think about. My gouging left a small, naked hole—big enough, I thought (knowing all along it wasn't true), to let the disease out, small enough to prevent a new one from sneaking in.

In September my mother called Warren and me into the kitchen and told us that, starting in seven months, the two of us would probably have to share a room for a while unless we wanted to sleep with a crying baby. Though I heard what she said, the meaning didn't register. I stood waiting, my brother silent at my side. She took a deep breath and began again.

"You see, I'm pregnant."

"Holy shit," said Warren, and she swatted the air in his direction, then flattened a hand on her stomach.

"Aren't you a little old, Ma?" I asked softly.

She turned her hand toward me, palm up. "We'll see if it looks like it'll come out okay. If it looks okay, we'll go ahead. People do this all the time."

"I can't share a room with him," I said. "I won't share a room with a guy."

And my mother said, "Kelly, he's your brother. I'm a little sick and tired of hearing nothing but whining around here. Can't you say something nice?"

I thought hard. "What'll you name it?"

"That all depends, stupid," said Warren, "on if it's a boy or girl."

They did tests of it inside her and it looked all right, and then it was spring and Adelaide Rose was born in perfect health, with arms like windmills, lungs like bellows, her cries filling the house. My mother took off two months from her job as an accountant and sat with the baby. Then in June Warren backed the car into a pole and made a four-hundred-dollar dent. A week later the orthodontist said that if I didn't have braces—at a cost of thousands—my jaw would be deformed. Also, the house was just too small; my brother and I were ready to kill each other stuck in one room together all the time. When school let out for the summer our mother went back to work to earn money for an addition to the house, for car repairs and my messed-up teeth. Our father worked, as usual, at the insurance office. Warren pumped gas. I got the baby.

Just for the mornings, she said at first, and then you can bike down to the pond, but her half-time job quickly turned full-time, mornings leaking into afternoons, and soon I was making lists to give my parents as they left for work: three boxes Luvs, two cases Enfamil, *Teen.*

"*Teen?*" my father said, squinting, and I glared at him.

"It's a magazine, Dad. To read."

Mornings, after the house had emptied out, I sprawled on the floor with the baby and looked at the photographs—the girls with wide, pink laughs or swollen pouts, their ponytails springing like fountains from their heads. They spent their days on camels' backs, these girls, or in open convertibles on blurry foreign roads. They moved. Over and over I told myself how it was all a lie, how in real life they were just models, bored and tired—how an electric fan, not the wind, was playing tricks with their hair. And yet still I wanted to trade places with those girls who always had something to do. Addie, too, was forever occupied, flailing her arms at insects or churning her legs in the air.

Sometimes, when the heat was more than I could take, I brought my sister to the bathroom, undressed us both, and stood with her under the shower. She would scream then, clinging to my small breasts as if they should yield something, her head dark and slippery as a seal's. I held her close and let her cry; the water cooled her down and then she'd nap. Some days we both fell asleep on a mattress in the damp basement like a family hiding from the enemy during wartime. I could kill an hour that way, sometimes two.

"Can't we switch?" I asked my brother at night through the sheet we had rigged on a string between our beds. "Just for a couple days? I can pump gas no problem. Warren?"

I sighed as loudly as I could. "You know I can pump gas."
He wouldn't answer, his back a shadow through the
sheet. "Warren?" I said. "I'm going nuts with her." But my
brother faked slumber or slept.

By midsummer Adelaide could hold her head up by herself and sit if I propped her up, so I began to take her out. I
found a large piece of cotton rag and rigged a sling for her,
tying her against my stomach and chest. I filled my knapsack with a diaper, bottle, magazine, and apple and stepped
into my sneakers, out into the dense air. Once, early on, I
tried riding with her on my bike, praying we would make it
the four miles to the pond, but as I leaned over the handle-
bars her weight unbalanced me so that I almost fell, and I
lurched forward, hands shielding her head, and swore at her
under my breath. Such a trusting head, there beneath my
palms—thin and brittle as an eggshell. I kissed her soft
spot, muttered that I hated her, and took her back inside.

Caroline, my best friend, had gone off to summer camp;
Jen was with her grandparents in the Catskills. Saturdays, I
biked to the pond and lay there on a towel drinking soda.
Across the way, skinny boys clung like monkeys to a long
rope swing, then dropped howling to the water. The talk on
the shore was of summer gossip, jobs at the 7-11 and at the
nearby camp, Monica dating some guy I didn't know. I tried
to join in, to laugh when the others laughed, but I couldn't
keep track of all the names.

"Your sister must be real cute by now," said Monica one
morning. She had visited Adelaide when she was born.

And I told her how the week before I'd been sitting with
Addie in the kitchen, about to give her a bottle, when she'd
made a noise, a b sound, which I could swear was the beginning of a word.

Monica was leaning over her thighs applying baby oil, her
skin shining. I realized she wasn't listening, and I heard my
own voice like the voice of my mother, coming from another world. I wanted to tell Monica how it wasn't that I

thought Addie was so special; I just didn't know what else to talk about. Instead I stopped in midsentence, and she squinted at the sky and told the clouds to get lost.

A hurricane would have pleased me that summer, or a locust swarm or small war. At night I watched the news on television: kids throwing rocks at tanks, a boat hitting an iceberg, a toddler named Cora Lee rescued from the bottom of a well. It seemed like part of a movie—the baby black with mud when they pulled her from the hole like an animal from its den, her teeth glinting, her eyes furious and bright. No one could ask her what she'd seen down there— she didn't know how to talk. Addie became my measuring stick, a signal of the passing time, for while the days and weeks crept sluggishly along, my sister grew at a frenzied pace and left a trail of outgrown sunsuits in her wake.

Weekdays, I walked the woods with her, this unexpected creature, pointing out the fit and ailing trees. I talked, not exactly to Addie since I didn't use her name or make my voice high and squeaky the way my mother did, but I decided I could speak out loud, since technically I was not alone. Some of the trees had long gashes in them, places where the sap was oozing out. Over these I placed leaves which stuck like pale green bandages—protection, I hoped, from insects and the drying effects of the sun. As the rays pushed through the sick trees, my skin freckled and burned, but Adelaide turned a color somewhere between golden and brown, her black hair growing like crabgrass in determined tufts upon her head. Sometimes I would unwrap her, set her down on the ground, and imagine leaving her there, for she had strong arms and legs, fierce lungs, and I could picture her making it just fine.

"See you, Addie!" I'd say over my shoulder, starting to walk off, and occasionally she would look up and let out an outraged wail, but more often she lay her head down on the bed of leaves, twitched her legs, and fell asleep. I would walk just to the point where I couldn't see her—sometimes a little farther—and then I'd go back, plop down next to her,

105

open my magazine. "Fun Ideas for Summer," I read for the third time: "Put lemon in your hair the next time you sit out in the sun; organize a vintage croquet game where everyone wears white; get in free swims by maintaining your neighbor's pool."

Sit with your baby sister in the woods and watch her sleep.

Sometimes, talking aloud to myself in the crackling woods, I began to lose my grip on things, my own voice amplifying, joined by a high-pitched ringing like an electrical noise, though there were no wires around. Then I would have to wake her up.

"Talk," I would command her, praying that a well-formed sentence would pop like a cartoon bubble from her mouth. "Say Kelly. Kelly. *Kel-ly*. Be a good baby. Stupid Addie. Want me to leave you here forever? Come on."

I bent over her and pulled down on her chin on the K, pushed it up for the *ly*. Adelaide opened her eyes, squinted in the sun. She smelled of dirt, the plastic of diaper, sour milk and spittle, the suffocating blend of powder mixed with sweat. Her nails were sharp, but her mouth was a smooth expanse of gum. She did not talk. When I had been tugging at her face for too long, she hunched her shoulders, getting ready to howl.

"Shush you, baby," I said, and I circled her cheek with my thumb and let her suck on my salty finger while I read.

My first orthodontist appointment fell on the third Wednesday in July. Warren, my mother decided, would stay home to watch the baby; my parents would drop me in town with my bike on their way to work. I dressed up for the occasion—a purple striped shirt, white Bermuda shorts—put my hair in a French braid on the slim chance that I would run into somebody interesting in town. The orthodontist cupped my face in his hand, slid freezing metal trays full of soft pink plaster into my mouth, told me to bite down. He leaned over me until I could see the under-

arm sweat patches on his white coat. His tan slacks
brushed my leg. I stared at the ceiling and tried not to move.

"Having a nice summer?" he asked, and through the cold
clamp of the mold I grunted, and he said, "Good, good."

Emerging from his office, I squinted and made my way to
my bike, running my tongue along my gums. I stopped for
a root beer, then drank as I rode one-handed down the narrow main street. I had the potholes memorized; where to
swerve left or right, where to plow ahead. When I got to a
straightaway, I closed my eyes for a few seconds—so quiet
inside my head, so cool and black, and such a perfect sense
of danger in riding blind. With my eyes squeezed shut I
could be anywhere, making my way down a road I didn't
know, exploring a new neighborhood after dark. The light
when I opened my eyes was so bright it hurt. When I got
home, Addie and Warren looked foreign to me, staring
strangers in a backwoods house.

"What's your problem?" Warren asked, because I was
hovering in the doorway. I shook my head.

"Addie shit her pants," said Warren, and she began to cry.

Every Wednesday morning my brother stayed home from
work and I got a series of hooks and wires cemented to my
wayward teeth. The rest of the time I walked with Adelaide
up and down the driveway, out into the woods. Everywhere, I was alert for signs of life: the squeal of the mail
truck's brakes, a soda can, the casing from a shotgun shell
lying half-hidden in the brush. Sometimes the tree men
parked their jeep at the cul-de-sac where our driveway began, and I crouched with Addie by the garage and spied as
they got out—one or two of them, sometimes three, holding clipboards and olive drab bags. Once my sister began
crying just as the motor went off, and I clamped my hand
over her mouth, startling her into silence so that all I could
hear was the tic-tic of the engine, and one of the men going
on about quadrants and marking space.

One day when the jeep was there, I dressed Addie in a red

terry suit, dressed myself in an orange T-shirt and white shorts, slung her across my front, and walked into the woods.

"We'll find one of the men," I said to my sleeping sister as I fluffed her hair, "and tell him that if he doesn't stop wrecking the forest we'll leave you with him, just like that, and he'll have to take care of you until he dies."

I remembered the fairy tales my grandfather used to read to me, of changeling children abandoned among beds of rushes, put in the fumbling hands of giants, left to grow up in the paws of some dumb beast. I sang softly as we walked:

> The grizzly bear is big and wild;
> He has devoured the infant child . . .

In the heat, I could feel the straps of the knapsack growing wet on my back. I sang louder:

> The infant child is not aware
> It has been eaten by a bear.

Something sharp sounded behind me, and I swung about. One of the tree men stood with a broken stick in his hands, laughing.

"Nice," he said. "Didn't bargain on free entertainment."

I scowled and shifted my sister, holding her against my body like a shield. He was not much taller than I was, with a shock of extremely blond hair. He wore khaki pants and a dark green T-shirt. He might have been in his early or mid-twenties, but it was hard to tell.

"What're you—babysitting the neighbor's kid?"

I looked at her strapped across my front, her twitching mouth, her closed eyes with their thick fringe of lashes, the imperfect shape of her head I had cupped so often in my hand.

"No," I said. "She's mine."

"Aw, come on," said the man. "How old are you, anyway? Still in braces. Still in diapers, almost."

"Old enough," I said.

He put out his hand and stroked her hair. I backed away. "Cute little thing. How old is she?"

"Four and a half months."

"Quick—tell me the day she was born—exact."

I rolled my eyes. "March tenth."

"Fast on the draw. Well, then, where's her daddy? I bet I know her daddy if he hangs around here."

I tossed my head and said what I had heard my aunt say countless times about her husband. "He's here and there. Around."

He snorted, but looked at me quizzically. "I hope she ain't your kid, sweetie. You're too young to have a kid."

I turned away, but something stopped me, and I made my voice impressively hard and low. "Why are you killing our trees?"

"Oh, for Christ's sake. Your trees. Talk to Uncle Sam. Who said they were yours?"

"It's my house there." I pointed over his shoulder. "On the edge, by where you parked."

"Your folks' house? Did they complain about this?"

"My house. I complain. You could at least cut them down so we could plant some more. My baby'll grow up in a desert."

Leaning on a tree, his hands hooked in his belt loops, he told me to relax, it wasn't him, he just worked for the forest. It was those scientists who put God knows what in the trees, way back when. In the long run it was supposed to help them figure out the diseases. Anyhow, he said, what did he know—he just went around and looked at the red dots and said if the leaves looked green or yellow.

"Tough job. I could do that," I said, thinking of my months of sabotage, and he said, "Not with your kid there, you couldn't. We cover lots of ground."

Addie tensed her legs the way she did when she was about to go, so I unwrapped her, put her on the ground, and began to rummage for a diaper. She made small noises, her skin spotted by the light, her eyes and mouth screwed shut.

"Quite a face she's got on. Hey there, raisin-head," he said, peering down at her.

"Yeah, well hold your nose."

I caught her ankles in one hand, undid her playsuit and diaper, and began swabbing at her with a tissue. The man kneeled next to me, gazed down at her red behind, her tiny cleft, so that I coughed and shifted to block my sister from his view.

"What's her name?" he asked as I taped her up and hung the dirty diaper from a branch to collect on our way home.

"Gloria."

"And yours?"

"Same thing."

"Pete Marcus here." He smiled. "Glad to meet you, Glorias. Pretty damn boring in the woods. Nice to run into some company."

I managed something between a nod and a shrug.

"You come here often?"

"Every day. I teach her Nature. We count the sick ones." He laughed. "How many?"

I made a wide circle with my arms. He stood up and began to measure a tree's girth, marking something on his clipboard.

"What're you doing now?" I said, scooping up Addie and tying her into her sling.

"Just seeing how much she grew since last time."

"And?"

"Dunno. I write down numbers. They do all the comparing back at the station."

"Not much, I can tell you that. It didn't grow hardly at all. It used to be one of the red dot ones. It's empty."

I struck it with my foot, almost expecting it to echo inside.

"It's not a red dot one. There's no red dot."

"Wait and see," I said, and turned to go.

"Hey, Glorias," said the man, Pete Marcus. We swung around. "Sit and have some lunch with me—she should like that. Come on and have a picnic in the woods."

And because I had not spoken to anyone except my family and orthodontist in a week, I unraveled my sister again and leaned with her against a tree. Pete squatted and pulled out a bologna sandwich which he tore in half. I fished for Addie's bottle.

"She doesn't, you know, get it from you?" he asked as I sat down, tilting her so she could drink.

I shook my head, appalled. "Nobody does that anymore."

It was clear he didn't have children, hardly knew what to do with them, the way he stared at her and reached out so tentatively to touch her arm, as if it held a potential shock.

"He dark?"

"Huh?"

"Her daddy. Is he dark?"

"Part Indian."

Pete Marcus bit into his sandwich and settled down next to us, and then, his mouth half full, he started to tell me how he wanted kids someday, and I should count myself lucky because sometimes you almost get something and then it disappears.

"Yeah," I said, thinking of my summer taken from me in one fell swoop.

"You know that song, 'I Had Me a Girl, Then My Girl Had Me?'" He started humming.

I shook my head and gave Addie a burp.

"I had me a girl, and overnight she turned into an ice cube. That's not how the song goes. Now she sure has kids—fill up a whole shopping cart. Must be banging away like bunny rabbits. Big old house they built, over in Ashland. Hey, I'm not, I don't know, shocking you or something, am I?"

I rolled my eyes again.

"Mostly I figure it's timing," he went on. "I figure that sometime, you know, way back during the cavemen or whatever, there was the perfect one just waiting for me, only she died way too soon, or maybe she's not born yet, or else she's too young." He pointed at Addie. "I like them dark. Maybe that's her, huh?"

Then he looked at me. "You find what you were after?"

I thought back on my fourteen years, but they seemed as clear and vacant as if I'd never been born, so I tried to empty the house of my true family and put a new one in. It had to be a young family, the parents still almost kids. Summer nights, before it got too dark, we'd all go down to the cul-de-sac and play Capture the Flag, Sardines, and Spud. I could picture the mother, tall and leggy like the models in my magazines, her brow wide, her eyes calm as the pool of water in the birdbath we had out back. There had to be a husband, too, but when I tried to imagine one, all I could come up with was a sixteen year old who looked vaguely like my brother, leaning toward the mirror in his underwear, examining his face for a trace of beard.

"I don't know," I said.

"Well, at least you got her."

And then he was leaning over and pressing his face to mine, the roughness of his chin scraping me, his tongue creeping into my mouth so that I shut my eyes and backed up against the tree, tasting bologna and something sour. I felt my eyes fill with tears, Addie asleep like a thick rag doll in my lap, the wires on my braces tugging at my teeth, the poplar hard against my spine. The magazines told you to eat parsley and mints, to carry a toothbrush in your purse. Such feeble, small advice, so lacking, but if I had known what was coming I might have tried. After what seemed like a long time, he pulled back and shook his head.

"Huh, I guess we're both a little lonely," he said, and then, noticing my tears, my fists clearing off my face: "Hey, you—aw no, Gloria. Nothing to cry about, for God's sake."

I bent over my sister, rubbed at her cheek which was smudged with dirt, then resettled her in my lap. I swallowed several times, trying to send back my tears, send back the lie which had come to me like a truth and clung to me like the creature in my lap, hard to get rid of, equally hard to keep.

"She's not mine," I said. "She's my mother's."

He reached over and touched her again, less hesitant this time, wrapping his hand around her ankle.

"Yeah," he said, and stroked her arch so that her toes curled around him like fingers. "I figured."

So I told him how I was almost fifteen and had never gone out with anyone, not even held hands, even though I didn't think I was so awful looking—or anyhow I hoped not—but I always had to be home doing stuff or taking care of the baby, and anyhow there was nobody to meet in this stupid crappy town.

"Hey no, you're real pretty, Gloria," he said, and pushed the sweaty hair which had come loose from my braid away from my face. "I'm not worried about you. Your time'll come. There are plenty of folks around for you."

I placed my hand over his on my forehead. My arm was trembling, but I traced his nails, the lengths of his fingers, his wide wrist, the way it seemed to me I should. He raised his other hand and lifted mine off. He reached for his lunch bag, crumpled it into a tight ball, and began tossing it from palm to palm.

"Listen, I shouldn't have done that, just then," he said. "Let's just pretend that didn't happen, just like we'll pretend you didn't make up stories about your sister there."

"I hate her," I said, looking down at Addie, but there she was, fast asleep, and I knew that no matter what I said, really she was mine, and that when she was grown and thought back, however vaguely, to her dim beginnings, it would be my arms she would feel carrying her through the poplar trees. That when she lifted her mouth and made sucking motions like a fish, I was the body she was gasping for, my tiny, milkless breasts.

"Now why would you go and hate her?" said Pete. "She's awful small to hate."

"Hold her," I said. "You can hold her if you want."

He put out his hands, and I placed Addie in them.

"Hey there, baby," he said, staying as immobile as he could. "Hey you."

And I leaned over her and tried to kiss him again, not sure how to go about it, sticking my tongue out first in an attempt to part his lips.

"No," he said, jerking his chin away, raising Addie up a few inches as if to push me off, then realizing his hands were tied by her. I sank back, rocking on my haunches.

Help me, I wanted to say. *Just show me what to do.* I pulled up a piece of prince's pine, then flung it to the ground.

"You're going to get us in real trouble, honey," he said. "I could be your father, almost. I'm way too old for you."

And I wanted to tell him that it didn't matter, that age in the middle of the woods like this had nothing to do with anything, that time had nothing to do with anything, just an expanse of blank before lunch, then after lunch, then before. I wanted to tell him that all I needed was a little something, a tiny bit of change to poke a pinhole through my summer so that I could see through it—a small hole so that some air could reach through the heat and clear things out.

He thought I didn't understand anything, too young, and so I played the part and took my sister back, abruptly, so that she squirmed and let out a cry. I nodded and said, "Yeah, you are too old," and when he laughed, probably halfway hoping I meant it as a joke, I looked at him straight on and asked him, "What?"

"Nothing, Gloria, nothing," he said. "Hell, this is some lunch break. Usually it's just me and the squirrels."

"Me too," I said. "Me and the squirrels and her."

"You take care, now, you hear?" he said, slinging his bag over his arm and rising to go. He leaned over to give my shoulder a careful pat, then touched Addie on the cheek.

"What'll you two do for the rest of the day?" he asked.

"Hang around," I said.

Then he was gone, or anyway he thought he was gone, but I wound Adelaide into her sling, and we followed him softly, watching the ground for piles of leaves and snapping twigs. Every time he stopped by a tree, we stopped behind another farther off, and if he knew we were there he didn't say anything, silent except for his whistling now and then, pieces of a song I didn't know. Once he stopped to scratch his back against a poplar like a deer and muttered something under his breath. Another time he took a canteen from his bag and poured water over his head until his hair turned a shade darker and dripped onto his shirt, leaving spots. Addie was not sleeping, but she did not cry. As we walked I ran my fingers in circles on her back the way she liked, to keep her still.

115

When he came to a red dot tree, Pete Marcus measured it like a dressmaker, winding his arms around it in a wide embrace, noting the measurements on his pad. Some of the trees had numbers assigned to them, engraved on tiny plaques like my father's army tags, just under the red dot. Some of the red dots were fading, and these he touched up carefully, as if he were doing someone's nails.

I followed him, watched him turn his head to scan for marked trees, counted as he passed by the ones I had already scratched out—some of the bare spots grown over now, some half scars, others still light and moist with sap, the nail holes visible where I had pried out the metal plaques. Each time he painted a new dot I waited a moment, then came up with Addie's extra diaper and wiped the wet paint away, noting the trees so I could come back later and check. All afternoon we followed him, undoing his work, undoing the work of the other tree men, the scientists, and Uncle Sam. It was not as if I thought it would do any good—the forest was turning empty inside, hollow as upturned toilet paper rolls; soon it would lean and fall. It was not as if I thought I was helping anything, but at least I could keep him wandering, this man who arrived in a large green jeep, who got into a large green jeep at the end of a sweaty afternoon and turned a key—such a simple thing—and drove away.

THE
BODY
SHOP

My mother had me sort the eyes. Blue in the biggest box, green in the middle, brown in the smallest box. She had me organize the hands: good, slightly damaged, very damaged, child's, woman's, or—that rare thing— man's. I screwed in legs, stood on an inverted bucket and dabbed paint at chipped neck joints.

"Get behind the ears, Simon," she told me as I stroked on paint. "Between the fingers, in the cracks." She mixed the sample flesh tones on an artist's palette, adding purples, greens—garish colors I couldn't imagine would transform into skin. And yet everything grew younger around my mother—the sallow became rich, the chipped became whole. Dull painted eyes were cut out with a razor and replaced with lambent glass ones; suddenly it was hard to stare back. Ten years old, I spent my afternoons tracing the facets of the body. Later, when slowly I began to encounter real flesh, the girls and women seemed off to me for a long time, too wide, too soft, all excess, evasion, and shifting eyes.

My mother had lovers. Businessmen, usually, but sometimes artists, and they were mad for her, all of them, arriving at the shop to steal a moment from her day, standing in a corner while she shone lights on her dummies and tested colors, her black hair cut short around her head like a boy's, her long hands splashed with paint. We couldn't stop watching her, my mother's lovers and I, perhaps because she rarely looked back.

To me, she barked commands in shorthand: "Mrs.

Revere at three—invoice, Simon. Spot check on wedding dress. Where is that goddamn polish? I told you, baby, polish on the blue shelf, would you just *try!*"

To the lover in the corner, she said little, but as she passed by with a wig or a coffee can full of paintbrushes, she would run a finger along the underside of his wrist or tap him, and then me, on the chin. A movie, dinner, the theater, they would offer, but she didn't like to leave me alone at night; the Adelsteins had had a break-in two years ago, and if Pammy hadn't hidden behind winter coats in the closet, everyone agreed she would have been stabbed or raped. Sometimes my mother invited the lover to the apartment. We sat then, the three of us, in the living room littered with lace ends and plastic fingernails. She grew quiet, thoughtful. She made me tell stories: "Tell him about the teacher who passed his gallstone around in class." "Tell the one about the frog and Mrs. Booth."

On first telling, when I was alone with my mother, I had delivered the stories with great aplomb. We had laughed until we choked, doubled over the workbench, calming ourselves with deep breaths and then meeting each other's eyes and starting up again. In front of my mother's lovers, my stories came out cold and thin.

"There's just this biology teacher Mr. Rodman," I would say, and my mother would squint and tuck in her chin, knowing I'd started out all wrong. After a while I did it on purpose, tired of my role as dancing monkey, tired of the men's stretched smiles and coughed-up laughs. Eventually, when my mother clapped her hands or yawned, I would be allowed to leave to do my homework. Nobody much wanted to talk anyway. Either she would usher the man down the front hall, saying she had to make an early start tomorrow, or else they would go into her bedroom and shut the door. Through the crack underneath her door would seep a nearly total silence; only a sneeze or a brief, amputated bark of laughter ever reached my ears.

"Sweet, that man," she would say absently in the morning, or, "Jesus, Simon lovey, I'm sorry I made you a boy. What a bunch of boors."

Then she would take out a marking pencil and give me a lesson, scribbling hurried, slanted letters on scraps of pattern paper. There were boors and there were bores and boars, just as there were holes and wholes, whiches and witches, friezes and freezes, nights and knights. Sometimes, my mother said, a talented person could beat the odds and be a boring boor.

The men never stayed overnight, for my mother had her own sense of propriety that surfaced now and then, and she must have thought I would get bad ideas. Also she needed her sleep. The business was growing, truckloads of tired mannequins arriving each week for face-lifts, special assignments for fashion shows, wedding parties, state gala events. We still shopped carefully, accustomed to a life of thrift, but my mother was making a way for herself in the world, making a way for me.

I liked the special orders best. They were the ones we got to dress, their skin tones calibrated to their outfits—tan beauties for the bathing suit sale, a ruddy Mrs. Santa, a pair of feverish children on skates. Only the fanciest stores demanded our services; the others couldn't afford our prices, didn't see the need for the refurbishment of their aging mannequins, for our special artistic touch. My mother could do anything, take a Basic—a female, stripped-down, unpainted base—and round it out with papier-mâché, clay, and wire until it was a buxom, glittering Mrs. Claus, one eye lowered in a wink. She didn't much like the stock or seasonal, preferring the stately or exotic, real challenges, one-timers: Count Dracula, Humpty-Dumpty, a young mannequin bride made to stand in the center of a fiftieth wedding anniversary gala wearing a dress long outgrown by its owner. We pasted the aging scalloped wedding photo over the workbench, and my mother made studied improvements—longer lashes, a smaller waist, buds of nipples to show faintly through the gauzy fabric of the dress. When

119

the plump and wealthy client stopped by each week to see how her former self was shaping up, my mother would steer her by the arm into the lovers' corner and tell her to stay quiet so we could concentrate.

With the increasing amount of money the shop was bringing in, she started a college fund, bought me educational toys, sent money to orphans in Israel and to help my alcoholic father in California—which was also like giving to a charity, she said. Chemistry sets and hand-carved chessboards gathered dust at home, for I worked in the shop after school each day, the way she had in her father's tailor shop.

"Rich, lazy boys are terrible creatures," she would tell me, but really she couldn't hold onto hired help, nobody up to her standards, nobody trained, the way I was, from birth. My toys stacked up in corners and became resting places for piles of fabric and skeins of colored yarn.

We worked hard, barely pausing for dinner. Each day I took the subway home from school, bought a candy bar for myself and one for my mother, and came directly to the store. In the evening, when the neighborhood turned dangerous, we lowered the metal grill over the shop window, fastened the police lock, and pulled down the green shade. Unless she had a man friend calling at our apartment down the street, we waited until our stomachs started rumbling too loudly to be ignored and then ate standing in the shop, Chinese food from the Magic Lantern next door. The dummies stood like naked female sentries, throwing confident, curved shadows about the room. At eight I began my homework while she kept on. We gave names, sometimes, to the ones we had been working on for a while. Miss Bridie for the wedding dress girl, Amber and Coffee-Tea-or-Me for the wispy bathing suit twins, Mr. Baby-They're-Playing-Our-Song for the debonair, tanned gentleman in a white suit.

As deadlines approached, the names got shortened: "Wrap up Mr. Baby, Simon. Put another coat on Coffee's lips."

One day she named a handsome dummy Frank, after my father, and kissed it on the forehead, and it came to me that she still loved him, that the checks and the long phone conversations in which she told him to get himself to a doctor—to get himself on unemployment, or would he like a ticket East?—were for herself as much as for him, probably more. I wouldn't refer to the mannequin as Frank, but called it by its official name: Invoice 304. I didn't want a father, didn't see the need. I was not unhappy—not after school, not on the weekends. At school I felt out of place and often missed my mother, but in order to leave the classroom behind, I had only to smell the turpentine on my shirt cuff or stare at my hands covered with nail polish, dots of paint, scabs of glue like a peeling second skin.

The last week in February my mother and I celebrated my eleventh birthday with a trip to the wax museum. Two days later class was dismissed early because of an approaching blizzard. The sky was gray and bloated, and though we had been instructed to go straight home, some boys were running off to play games in a vacant lot a block from school. For a moment I considered joining them, but I wasn't good at games, and, besides, I pictured my mother's surprise at seeing me early, how I would come in the back way and sneak up behind her with a mannequin arm, tickle her neck, and hear her scratchy laugh. I took the subway. By the time I had emerged from the dark tunnels, it had begun to snow. I ate my candy bar as I walked to the workshop, licking off the snowflakes as they dotted the chocolate with white spots.

When I got to the back door, I opened it carefully, then moved easily through the dark storeroom to the box of ladies' arms and separated one from the rest, sliding it out inch by inch so as not to clank. I sucked in my breath, tense with anticipation of my small joke, how the moment would approach and arrive, and then we would laugh about it afterwards, reenacting it until it became one of our nurtured private memories, one of the stories which fell flat before any but our own ears. As I crept toward the front workroom, I heard voices, hers and someone else's, a customer's.

"How many again?" she said, and he answered, "Hundreds for you, you do such a beautiful job. How do you get them so beautiful? Almost as pretty as you."

"Sweat," my mother said, "and broken nails."

I paused, knowing not to interrupt her with a customer, hoping she would mention my name: My son Simon helps every day after school. I couldn't do it without him.

"The thing is," said the man's voice, and by now I was leaning behind the doorway and could see the back of his dark suit, his bald head rimmed with a neat line of white hair. "The thing is we have the people in Queens who usually do it. For a good price, too."

"What people?" said my mother. "You're talking a shoddy paint job. Nobody does this the way I do."

"No," said the man. "No, probably not."

And then he was leaning toward her and whispering something in her ear, so that I wondered if I had been spotted and found out. My mother backed off, said, "Oh, for God's sake. This is a business I run here."

"Yes," said the man. "I know."

"Well, then?" said my mother.

And the man said, "For years I've had nobody, but I run a good and decent business."

"Me too, I run a good and decent business," said my mother, and he shrugged and started to walk off. My mother looked over toward the storeroom as if she were staring straight at me, and then she whispered something to herself, untied her apron, and lifted it over her head. She lowered her chin and began to unbutton her work shirt, then turned so the man could unfasten her brassiere, which he did with calm, efficient hands. She turned again and drew him to her, the back of his head disappearing from my sight as he lowered his face to her chest.

"This is it," she said.

I dropped the arm with a clatter, turned to run. As I

swiveled around I caught a glimpse of my mother's hands flashing toward me through the air.

"Simon!" she called, but I ran through the dark storeroom and out into the snow, and though I stood there for a minute catching my breath, half expecting her to show up at the back door, only silence issued from the building. As I started down the street trying to push the picture of my mother from my mind, other pictures came to me—the teenage couple in our neighborhood who rode a motorcycle, how the girl pressed up behind the boy, put her chin on his shoulder, and slid her hands into the waistband of his jeans. My father—the way, when I was almost too young to remember, he would call me in some mornings and let me crawl into bed with them, between their large bodies smelling of sleep. Then we would be sandwiches—pastrami, egg, roast beef. I would be the meat, and my parents, hugging each other around my skinny body, would be the bread, kissing and tickling my stomach and the back of my neck until I laughed so hard that once I actually wet the bed. I wasn't sure if I really remembered this, or if my mother had told it to me. Sometimes I doubted I'd ever had a father at all.

There were other things I was more sure of—the noises that came from my mother's room when she had guests there at night, the pride I felt at school open house when she was prettier than all the other mothers, a red scarf in her hair. I knew how to link the tiny metal catches on the tops of her dresses to close the collar, how to apply a thin, even coat of fingernail polish to the run on her stocking, how to scratch her back or her chin when her hands were covered with paint. My mother prided herself on being up front, and yet when I saw her there with the white-haired man, I had a feeling I knew nothing about her, about anything, the whole world operating in secret exchanges behind my back—even this mother who allowed her son no secrets, who scrubbed and questioned and drew out my insides until so much was on the surface that I wondered if anything could be left inside.

"I hate you," I muttered, turning down a residential side street, a cluster of cats scrambling out of my path. The snow was slippery, already turning brown. The vocabulary words we were learning that week in school began to run through my head like a dull song: *procrastinate, nonchalant, efficient, hypocrite.* That was the one I wanted. Balancing on someone's front stoop, I said it: "Hypocrite." I would say it again when I saw her, sneer if she didn't know what it meant. For she wasn't so smart, my mother, after all, and I was growing smarter every day.

When I got too cold, I went back to the store, back to the workroom, tiptoeing in case he was still there, but he was gone. My mother had put on her apron and begun to mix colors again.

"Simon," she said, and I kicked at the side of a work table with my boot. "I've asked you not to come in when I have a customer. You're home early, huh? Because of the snow?"

I looked at the ceiling.

"Can you believe how much it's snowing?" she asked. I stared at a web of cracks from a leak we'd had. "Maybe you can stay home tomorrow. It takes them forever to clear the roads."

My voice sounded inside my head, then came out. "Who was he?"

"Who was he? He was—he was just a man. Just a very important man who runs the period fashion show at the opera. They read our ad in the paper."

I took a deep breath. My mother looked a bit twisted to me, bent out of shape, as if someone had taken her apart and put her back together again slightly out of whack. Then I realized that she had buttoned her work shirt wrong, so that it hung crooked across her chest.

"Your shirt's a mess—" I said, pointing.

"Oh." She looked down and began redoing the buttons. "Yes. Thank you."

I stood with the snow melting off my boots in a slick puddle and watched her hands.

"Well," she said when she had finished buttoning. "He gave us a big account, baby. You feel like helping? I'm all ready to get down to work."

I shook my head, and she sighed and stepped toward me, but I backed away.

"What, are you mad at me, Simon? If you are, just say so. Are you, huh?"

I shook my head again.

"Oh, come on, honey," she said, and I could feel something stretching out, growing taut and panicked in her voice. "Let's just forget it, okay?"

I nodded, but we both knew I didn't mean it, and I could tell how badly she wanted me to open my mouth and say anything at all. I pictured a silver zipper on my mouth, closing it like stitches, sealing it from her. I kicked at the bench again and felt my mouth twist into a scowl. She pushed aside the palette she had been mixing on so that some globs of paint fell like bird droppings to the floor. She bent down and began attacking the paint spot with a sponge.

"Okay, fine," said my mother. "Go play baseball. Go play with the other kids."

As she scrubbed, she began to hum a cheerful tune. I started to back toward the front door, pledged to silence, but the zipper on my mouth gave way, and I found myself whispering "shut up bitch, shut up bitch" under my breath. My mother dropped the sponge and came after me.

"What did you say?"

"Nothing."

She grabbed my jacket collar, dug her nails into my neck. "What did you say, Simon?"

"Bye. I said bye." I had begun to cry, trying to squirm away from her.

My mother peered down at me, and in the narrowed slits of her eyes I saw a pure and concentrated disdain which made her hands tense up and her lips and the bridge of her nose grow tight and pale.

"Don't you ever lie to me," she said. "Do you hear me? Don't you ever, ever lie to your mother, you little bastard!"

"What I said," I told her, twisting out of her hold, "was 'shut up bitch'." I yelled it as she leaned over me, directly into her ear. "Bitch!" I tried to think of the vocabulary word I had used before, but it had slipped away.

My mother grabbed me again, slapped me hard across the cheek, and then she was pressing me to her apron, which smelled of turpentine, touching her mouth to my hair.

"Oh Jesus, baby," she said, and her torso shook so that I wondered if she had begun to laugh or cry. She rocked me, but I held myself rigid. "Some pair we are, the bitch and the bastard. What do you think the Adelsteins would say to that?"

I shrugged, and she let go of me, patted me on the behind. "Wow," she said. "I've never seen you get so mad. You've got quite a temper under there, huh? That's good. You're going to need it in this world."

And I felt her swiftly take it from me—my small arsenal of playground obscenities, my Temper—felt it change under her stamp of approval until it became flat and useless, no longer mine. Bitch, I thought, but the word sounded dull, like a rusty blade.

"We've got nothing but each other, kiddo, whether you like it or not," she said. "I love you to death. You have the afternoon off. Live it up, because tomorrow we get going on the costume show, if you still want to help."

As I started out the door, she called "Simon," and I turned.

"I don't expect *you* to be perfect," she said, and I thought of how many times that week she had made me redo the fingernail polish on a hand because I'd smeared the edges, or botched the color slightly, or let a brush stroke show.

"Okay, I expect a lot of you," she added, reading my mind. "But just to try your best, is all. No more."

I pictured her guiding the old man's mouth to her breast like a baby's, waving her hands as she saw me standing there. I turned again to leave.

"I *do* try my best," my mother called, and for the first time in my memory I thought she really was about to cry.

"You try raising a kid and running this lousy business," she said, and she gasped and let her jaw drop as if the air had turned to water and she couldn't breathe. As she reached out her hand to steady herself, the emergency medical number—911—flashed across my brain, but then she was standing straight again, dry-eyed, drawing in slow breaths.

"I—I was dizzy. I guess I'm a little upset," she said after a moment, then sighed. "Would you come and give your old Ma a hug?"

So I went and held her and thought how she wasn't so tall—I was catching up—and she wasn't as pretty as she used to be—all the little lines on her neck and around her eyes. But still, somehow, I didn't want to leave her for a neighborhood full of strange kids and games I hardly knew how to play.

"How many?" I asked her, and she said, "It's a windfall, sweetie. Ninety-five women, twenty kids, ten men. It'll be gorgeous, in the lobby of the opera hall. Spring tones, and the supply budget is enormous. They want a Queen Victoria, and Mary What's-her-name—Queen of—"

"Scots."

"Just testing. The royalty in the center, and then the handmaidens in a circle, and the children on the stairs going up."

Her eyes were shining; she had begun to wave her hands. We would have to clear out work space, bring in the barrels to mix uniform lots of flesh paint. We would have to organize ourselves.

"It's snowing," I said. "Nobody plays baseball in the snow."

And my mother took my hand as if she'd known that all along and led me to the musty storeroom to gather parts.

Twice a week I went to see my mother at the King David Residence for Jewish Elders, a stately nursing home where she sat with her one leg, the other gone to gangrene below the knee a few years back, and cancer running races through her remaining bones. Saturdays, I brought my daughter Rebecca, nine years old and a beauty, although she didn't quite know it yet. In my mother's private room we perched among fabric scraps and ribbons, and my mother gave Rebecca gifts—a feathered hat, a ten dollar bill with "For My Treasure" written in block letters on the portico of the U.S. Treasury, a piece of lace to weave through her braid. Rebecca was in the best schools, doing well; my mother was receiving top-notch care. Still, they found much to complain about. The man who fit her prosthesis kept feeling up her thigh, said my mother, and when I motioned at my daughter, she said, "Oh shush, Simon. Why not teach her early what to watch out for? With her looks, they'll be all over her like flies."

Rebecca complained that she didn't win the singing prize at school, though she was sure she had the best voice.

"Of course you do," said her grandmother. "The judges must be deaf."

The two of them criticized the food, the smell of disinfectant. They bitched. As they grew more animated, their displeasure became a sort of cockeyed joy; their nostrils flared, they made wide paths with their hands. I watched. When Rebecca went down the hall to beg Jello off the nurses, my mother gestured for me to come closer, put her hand on my knee, and asked me how Kimberly was.

"Would you just ask your granddaughter, Mom," I said. "You know I'm no expert."

For three years I'd been divorced, and for three years she'd asked me how Kimberly was as often as she dared, usually once or twice a month.

"When you pick your daughter up and drop her off, you must see something," she said, and I wondered what she expected from me, expected from this ex-wife of mine whom she could never get along with, both of them too fiery to make a proper mix, and myself placed between them like a piece of shade. Weekends, when I dropped my daughter off and picked her up, I got no farther than the corner. When, rarely, Kimberly called me, it was because she was, in her words, so lonely she could die, just jilted, or because the harp concert she gave got a lousy review, or because Rebecca had expressed interest again in moving in with me.

Then my ex-wife and I met in parks and cafés and soothed each other with the familiar odd gesture—hair smoothed away from a forehead, a squeezed hand, a slipped-in kiss. Or rather I soothed her. Staying angry was beyond me, though I had my ways and tempted my daughter to the apartment with expensive stereo equipment, a lack of regulations, an overabundance of her favorite food. I had fixed it up since the days I'd lived there as a boy, knocked down walls, installed a skylight. The neighborhood was growing gentrified. I had painted Rebecca's room, formerly the sewing room, a rose faux-marble. My own room I left white.

My mother said, "I just don't want you to be alone. Is there someone else? "

I shook my head no. Only the business—the decorative art, marbleizing and trompe l'oeil jobs I did in luxury apartments, restaurants, and hotels—so much more than I could keep up with, an excess of money, of clients. I had become quite skilled at painting, though I still could not paint people—only flora, fauna, imitation stone. A few months earlier I had been featured in a slick magazine with a picture of the lake I painted on the floor of the Restaurant des Cygnes. I showed the article to my mother, and she held it up to the light, her eyesight weak.

"Yes," she said. "Yes. Fine. Lovely. You'd better make the clients take off their shoes when they go in there, or it'll be ruined in no time."

"There are mirrored paths," I said. "I'll take you there sometime for dinner." And she blew air out of her mouth with a whistling sound and gestured dismissively at her false leg.

She asked me did I need money, for Rebecca, her school,

for myself, a treat. "No," I said. "I'm fine." Always the same thing.

"I'd slip that prosthesis man a check," she said, "if he'd only keep his hands to himself."

I looked away, and she said, "You don't believe me, Simon. Have I ever lied to you? He must be a sick man, maybe on drugs or something, the way his hands shake."

I didn't want to think about it, so I went down the hall to retrieve Rebecca, and then we wheeled my mother to the flagstone patio and sat staring at the small pond. The stooped and hobbled residents were everywhere; my mother waved and called to them by name. Most of them adored her, for her energy, her wit. The old men left gifts outside her door, and each week she took the objects from a drawer and tried to give them to Rebecca or me—chocolates, a deck of cards, a faded Rosh Hashanah card.

"Their children give them presents," she said, "and they give the presents to me, and then what am I supposed to do?"

Some people at the residence disliked my mother, jealous, she said, of the son who visited twice a week and the fact that she had gotten her money from her own hard work, not from the sweat of others or her husband's pocket, and because her granddaughter was the loveliest one around. Rebecca skipped on the lawn, balanced with extended arms on the edge of the concrete pond, and I called out to her to be careful or she'd fall.

"Leave her be," said my mother. I called out again, louder this time, and Rebecca turned, lost her balance, and plunged one sneakered foot and a blue-jeaned leg into the shallow pond.

"Oh shit!" she yelled, then clamped her hand over her mouth as the people stared. My daughter went to her grandmother's room, where she knew how to find things. When she joined us again she was wearing a striped skirt of my mother's, down to her ankles and held up with a sash, and Chinese peach silk bedroom slippers laced with gold thread. She pranced in front of us and made a face.

"Oh no you don't! You put that dry sneaker back on your left foot to leave me one clean slipper," said my mother. "But thank you for falling so conveniently. What do I need with the right one anyway?"

We drove to the Botanical Gardens and took a walk. Pushing the wheelchair through so much cultivated green, I found myself dizzied by the pollen, by the soft earth which gave way beneath my feet, the garden mazes of shaped hedges and flowering trees.

131

My mother pointed things out to us: gardenia, flowering maple, bachelor buttons, clematis, weeping cherry tree. Rebecca remembered them from last time, though she never quite seemed to be listening. She anticipated answers, pointed and ran in circles, recited names back. I followed in my head, but they were too quick for me—another world altogether out there with all those green and growing things. I ran through names of pigments in my mind as I saw the colors in the unfamiliar flowers: alizarin crimson, cerulean blue, rose madder, burnt umber, venetian red.

"Poppy," said Rebecca, and I saw lampblack crouched in its center like a spider.

Half listening to their talk, I made a mental list of decorative painting methods: stippling, combing, dragging, mottling, pouncing, rag rolling, tuffbacking, decoupage, frottage. Most of it I had taught myself. I rested my hand on my mother's head, stroked her hair, still so soft. She closed her hand around mine, and we stopped for an instant while Rebecca ran on ahead.

"Hi," I said to my mother.

"Baby," she said.

Such a secret, juvenile pleasure I took in the fact that my mother did not know the shoptalk of my trade.

This morning she died, my mother. It was bound to happen sometime. I know that, I tell myself that: just as everybody has a mother, everybody's mother dies. We are having a cold spell; inside, the air is static, crackling with heat. My daughter, who is with me for the weekend, sits quietly as I tell her, then goes to her room and shuts the door. I leave her there in the apartment where I grew up and go for a walk on the winter streets. Krugel's is having a fur sale. The women in the window are naked underneath their minks, the joints of their wrists showing, their eyes flat and dull as slate. I have not kept up the mannequin business, though I still get calls from ex-clients now and then: a nativity scene, a pair of lovers, a fife and drum corps. I say no.

If I were my mother, I could replace her body part by part—a plastic leg, a glass eye, skin mixed from a slew of gaudy colors, hair tinted with a supple brush. I could mix and match, scrape and barter, make do. But I am not my mother, and loss comes to me whole and unwieldy, as awkward as the bulky man in the overcoat who looks out at me from the shop window, eyes level with the fur-clad women's jointed waists. What, I wonder, have I become? What has she made of me with such careful pruning, such close directives, such proximity to all she knew as true? A stringy knot of reproach begins to tie itself in my gut that she has not done better, made more of me, made me more— a woman of her talent, energy, and skill. I have not come out feeling particularly grown, though I do feel old. I expect myself to be smaller, wish myself smaller, but the man I see is overweight, no youngster, brow furrowed, chin weak, face clouded by the condensation of the cold.

"You're a details person, is what you are," my mother told me when I was a boy. "You go ahead with the lashes and fingernails and leave the rest to me."

I think for a moment about her money piled on top of my own, what a rich man I have just become, how, if I liked, I could never work another day in my life, how I could stay by my daughter's side. I think of my mother watching Rebecca by the water, telling me to leave the child be. What, I wonder, would she have done if I had been the one playing on the edge, and still a clumsy boy? I was not that sort of child. It is not a good idea, I realize, to go home just now; I should learn to leave my daughter to herself and her salty grief.

I begin to walk, and the windows are full of bodies, most of them poorly rendered, awkwardly posed in the evening light. I cannot look without correcting, patching a joint here, a chip there until I reach the end of the street. A details person, said my mother, but already the details begin to slide from me. I am not sure where to go from here, so I turn and make my way slowly back on the other side. My thoughts are critical—I see only the shoddiness, the carelessness, the way a woman's arm in the window is bent as if she broke it, her foot curved as if caught in a lifelong cramp.

What I cannot do, my weak point, is create a perfect window world, the figures poised like bits of grace, their mouths on speech's threshold, their eyes on the edge of sight. It is not that it cannot be done—I've seen it—but I cannot do it myself. For a moment I imagine bribing the Krugel's security guard to let me into the window; I would bring along a palette, some tubes of paint, some glass eyes. Then I would do my best to transform the fur-clad women into graceful, happy creatures—I'd bend their arms into motion and provide them with new eyes. But my daughter is home alone, and these days in the city a security guard would probably shoot me in the head. Anyway, they are nothing but mannequins, and I am nothing but a bulky man in an overcoat, growing colder and colder as I walk along until my lungs hurt from the mere act of breathing, and I can think of nothing but getting warm.

MUSIC FOR
FOUR
DOORS

Mornings, I know that he'll be standing there, staring at the flower in my yard. As I step onto the porch and lower myself into the wicker chair, Daniel will be sinking to his knees, peering at the deep blue buds of the platycodon. As I scan the street and pile my books on the railing, he'll squint. At the glossy, pointed leaves? At an ant zigzagging a stem? At something only he can see? The look on his face is always the same—the thick, concentrated attention of a scientist staring into a microscope, only more fixed and somehow also more blank. Usually he doesn't notice when I appear.

For me every morning is different. A heel wakes me, presses against my bladder; the next day something shifts— knee, elbow, hand? There are mornings when I wake full and happy. "Feel," I say to Thomas, next to me in bed. At first his hand was tentative, as if he were petting a wild animal for the first time. Lately he has grown easier, rubbing almond oil in circles on my stretched skin. Other times it is as if I have insects forming ranks around my middle—waking me, nibbling me, reminding me that my time is not my own. Go away, get out, I think, to the movement inside me, to the man beside me, who sleeps flat on his stomach with his legs splayed, his mouth slightly ajar. Through all my changes, his body has stayed totally unchanged.

For Daniel who visits my flower, every morning needs to be the same. His mother, Katherine, has told me of his rituals: how he arranges his magic markers in a spectrum, places his drinking glass in the same spot in the same cupboard every night, lines his shoes up in perfect marching order, wakes to his clock radio set to the same moment on the same station: "Seven o'clock and time to shine! WKZY!!" If someone jumbles up his markers, if the radio station allows a song to run through the announcement of seven o'clock, if the glass is switched with another or a shoe kicked aside—if chaos nudges order (and a nudge, it seems, is all it takes), Daniel has a fit.

I've heard it from next door—shrill, rhythmic, staccato yelps. Then silence. Those mornings, Daniel does not come to see my flower or walk by the house on his way to sort mail at the post office, lunch bag and umbrella in his hand. Those mornings, Daniel's mother does not go to work at her part-time job. Sometimes, as the day wears on, she'll come over and sit with me, craning her neck toward her own house now and then.

"He's under his quilts," she said once when I asked if she needed to get back. "He's okay. He'll come out when he's ready to come out."

It seems that anything can set him off. He might come across a stamp a coworker at the post office has forgotten to cancel, or notice that a vase has been moved to a different table, or answer a phone call in which the caller neglects to say, "This is _____, may I please speak to _____?" Dust in the corners can do it, a buzzing in the air, things we see and do not see, the mess of the visible and invisible world. It seems he is a synapse, this man in my yard, a spliced nerve, its ending quivering and raw.

My flower. If there is pleasure for someone like this, if pleasure is something he can know, then I am sure my flower pleases him. I have many flowers; the platycodon is neither the brightest nor the most spectacular, but it is one of the oddest, its bud inflated and boxy like a Chinese lantern, its flower bell-shaped where most blossoms flare open like trumpets or bowls. In China, where it comes from, they call it a balloon or bell flower. When kneeling was no effort, I spent my weekends on this ground, tamping annuals into the resistant New England soil, adding peat moss, manure, lime. Next to my new plants the old poked their way through, flowers put in by other people before we got here: irises and daylilies, phlox and lilies of the valley. The platycodon was the only one I didn't recognize, but I thumbed through my gardening book until I found its picture: *Platycodon grandiflorus blue.*

Thomas would join me sometimes and stand far back from the beds as if afraid of the power of his own feet. "What's that one?" he'd ask. "What's that?" My nails would get caked with dirt, the knees of my jeans turn slick and brown. I'd sift the grainy soil, forbidden to me as a child, down through my fingers and watch it change the color of my hands. Worms showed up in the dirt and slid, obscenely pink, across my skin. I never understood how they managed to stay so clean.

Daniel doesn't notice the zinnias, the English daisies, the silver and blue pinwheels I have stuck in the soil for his benefit, or the cloth bags of human hair I have hung from the bushes (Katherine's grandmother's remedy) to keep away rabbits and woodchucks. More than that, he doesn't notice me, though I am larger than the flowers and more talkative. Oh, he knows me by name, can say, "Hello, Carlotta, I have brought you *Ladies' Home Journal,*" and hand up a magazine, but his voice is like a radio being spun between stations, every word cutting itself off to be replaced by another. Every word oddly untethered and alone.

There are ways to define us. He is autistic. I am pregnant. Soon I will no longer be pregnant. Then I will be other things again—retrieve the bits of myself that have grown small and distant as my belly grows: lover, journalist, friend. And mother—that, too. Mostly I dislike these definitions, though I am grateful that more than one applies to me, that over the years they have built up in a small pile. Daniel will always be autistic; never, probably, lover or father. Though he must be in his mid twenties, he looks like a delicate squinting boy, his skin clear, his hair glossy, his fingers long and thin.

My ankles swell, then my wrists and hands; my wedding ring tightens on my finger. I worry about eclampsia, get my blood pressure checked, give them my urine, the plastic of the full sample cup warm to my touch. Normal, they say, but still they warn me to stay quiet. I have miscarried once before, two years ago, in a different town, and though I've made it past that danger point this time, premature delivery is still a threat. Avoid unnecessary movement, I am told. Avoid unnecessary stress. I must not sit before the computer screen and work on an article; the magnetic field could damage the unborn fetus. I don't drink wine—fetal alcohol syndrome. I've never smoked, and I don't smoke now, but somehow knowing that I shouldn't makes my hand grasp for phantom cigarettes. I chew on cinnamon sticks instead.

In this dangerous, or should I say anxious world, I sit on my front porch like a woman from another era. Nearly everyone has gone to camp or work or summer school. I go nowhere, sit on my porch like the watchwoman, the neighborhood gossip, but mine is a ghost neighborhood by day. Such a shame, for I could pick up on a great many things from here. People have hitched their dogs to run lines and left their sprinklers on. I sit on the porch—each day the same place, each day a different body—and watch the sprinklers work their way across hedgerow, sidewalk, lawn, hedgerow. The dogs run back and forth along their scraping chains.

I watch Daniel. I see him leave for work and know it is fourteen minutes till eight. I see him return from work and know it is three-fifteen. His mother has told him to bring me magazines from the unclaimed heap at the post office, so each day at three-fifteen, Daniel hands me one. This, aside from Thomas coming home, is the highlight of my day. Sometimes he brings me standard fare—news or fashion magazines. Other times, as he bends over the pile, his hand lights on stranger things: *Trailer Boats Magazine, Lefthander Magazine, Llamas Magazine: The International Camelid Journal, St. Joseph's Messenger and Advocate of the Blind.* One day he hands me something wrapped in brown paper—pornographic stories of mystery and suspense. I read about female spies with body parts like ripe melons, split pomegranates, swollen cherry buds. Do the spies, I wonder, feel as I do—that they're about to burst open, that in bursting, they might self-destruct?

The magazines make me peer down the street with a new wonder, a sense that, despite my curiosity, I have been missing something. I thought I knew this small town: as a reporter you can learn a lot in a year—not only streets and the names of the secretaries at the town hall, but town hates and prides, feuds and prejudices, which son made the hardware store go bankrupt, which business pushed another off the block. Never once did I see a llama walking down the street. Thomas is editing the business supplement and stays late at work. When he gets home he massages my feet and asks me about my day. A llama can cost $45,000, I tell him, and he asks what kind of mileage they get.

After dinner, refinishing an old cradle, he finds a carving underneath the thick paint, two birds with their wings above a star.

"Look at this," he says. "It's probably hundreds of years old. Is that beautiful or what?"

I nod and smile, but my head is throbbing, and I can feel my smile strain.

"What?" he says. "What, Carlotta?"

I cannot tell him what; I hardly know. He kicks the cradle so it rocks. Then, when still I do not answer him, he kicks it harder until I am afraid he will overturn it or put his foot right through the wood.

"Don't," I say. "You'll ruin all your hard work."

He stops kicking and lets a piece of sandpaper fall to the floor.

139

"You know," he says, "I uncover this thing, this—carving—and I get excited, and you just stand there looking at me like I'm from Mars. Can't you get a little excited, or is that totally inappropriate?"

"I *am* excited," I tell him. I am. At the same time, I'm a penny tossed from a skyscraper, spinning, about to bore a hole through pavement, or a passenger on a runaway train. Or no, perhaps I am—my body is—the train itself. Miracles are miracles, but this thing is in my belly, and I cannot stop it. Not that I would want to, I would not want to, but the fact is I can't.

Daniel was the second child, an easy birth. When she first saw him, Katherine was startled by his beauty; he had no wrinkles, rashes, or spots where her body had pressed up against his and left marks. Later, she was surprised by how quiet he was. Her other son had squalled, but Daniel was silent in his crib. His parents clapped near his ears to make sure he wasn't deaf, waved hands before his eyes to make sure that he could see. Then they noticed he wasn't learning to walk and didn't speak, not a word out of his mouth. But as he grew older he did react to things. If you tried to caress him, he locked his joints and stiffened his body like a board. If you changed the nipple on his bottle for a fresh one, he shrieked and clamped his hand over his mouth.

His parents worked with him—mostly his mother; his father was a lawyer and not often home. He learned to walk and talk, to count. He counted stairs. He counted slices of bread, pins, the knotholes on the boards of the pine floors. He added, subtracted, multiplied, and divided, far beyond his years, but he didn't have conversations and couldn't tell a stranger his own name. Slowly his mother came up with a system of rewards and punishments. Daniel walked around with a little red plastic counter like the ones old women use in grocery stores to calculate their bills. "If someone says, 'Hello,'" his mother taught him, "you say, 'Hello.'" "If someone says, 'Thank you,' you say, 'You're welcome.'" Daniel would say "you're welcome," click himself a

140

point. Fifty points and he'd get a reward—some new pastels or a visit to a construction site where a house was going up. He'd sit for hours watching as the rafters got filled in. They put him in the special education class at the public school but within a week he'd thrown a chair at a smaller boy, so the teachers sent him home. His mother taught him to read and write, wash dishes and bake bread. He drew pictures: close-ups of clock radio dials, window grids, the corner of his parents' living room, or the bristles of his toothbrush, seen from above. Later, when it became the law, the school took Daniel back. He memorized the planets and made drawings of the sky above his house at night, the constellations represented with the accuracy of a stellar map.

"How old are you?" Katherine asks me, sitting on the porch, and when I tell her thirty, she nods. "Same as Daniel," she says, and I feel a shock. Though I knew he was no boy, I have been thinking of him, still, as a peculiar child—the child I might bear, must avoid bearing by having generous thoughts and sitting like a wicker statue in this wicker seat. Now, when I find he is my age, he becomes, quite suddenly, the child I might have been.

I always thought I'd like my baby to wear shoes only in winter. I thought I'd like it to sleep in a big wooden box and wear T-shirts and tights instead of prim dresses or sailor suits, to play in the mud, get mud beneath its fingernails, roll dirt over its tongue, eat with its hands when it's hungry, stay up until it wants to sleep. A life without rules, so she, he, could grow up flexible and sturdy, not like a platycodon with its deep tap root, so difficult to transplant, but like a morning glory: wherever you put it, it takes root.

This was my plan, but places in Sweden, Norway, San Francisco, and New York keep sending us glossy catalogues, as if news of my belly has spread around the world. There are car seats and crib bumpers, videos for training babysitters on emergency care and first aid. Breast pumps, electric squawk boxes so you can hear your child crying in another room, straps for the stroller, gates for the stairs, covers for the outlets, locks for the cabinets and doors.

The larger my body grows, the larger I wish my mind would grow with it, only I'm shrinking, I'm so scared. From the walls the faces of the three-pronged outlets stare at me: black eyes and deep electric mouths. It must be more like a prison than a home, the domain of those first few years. To wake in a slatted bed and get moved to a harnessed chair, no object near you, ever, except what's too big to fit inside your mouth. I think of newborn rabbits tumbling underground, dirt on their skin, or human babies in other parts of the world, slung on their sisters' backs or left to nap among the livestock in the yard. Is it that, in these parts, we humans are more delicate, or have we booby-trapped our world until we must shield our offspring from our own inventions by making new inventions that protect?

You have too much time to worry, sitting home alone, Thomas tells me, Katherine tells me, even my mother tells me over the phone. I practice my breathing exercises— slow breaths, quick breaths, panting, blowing, puffs. I do my pelvic tilts. I fall asleep late and wake early every morning now, long before Thomas, long before Daniel goes to work. One day in the afternoon (I am due in six days, though I never know whether to believe those numbers), Daniel stops by the flower and kneels, and I leave the porch to go stand by him.

"Hi, Daniel," I say. He doesn't seem to hear. "Hi, Daniel," I repeat, and he looks up.

"Hello, Carlotta."

"How was work today?"

"Work today was fine, thank you."

"Lots of letters?"

"Yes."

"Do you like my flower?"

He juts his jaw forward. "Platycodon."

"I know. It's pretty, isn't it? I think it grows better because you give it so much attention."

He turns to me, his fists clenched at his sides. "Household animals can be put in a hazardous position without your even knowing. You must run a tight house and guard your precious pet from the dangers of suffocation, leash hangings, food poisoning, and death by automobile."

His voice is automatic, like a computer's. I laugh. "What are you saying, Daniel? Did you read that somewhere? At work maybe?"

He stares down at the plant again, transfixed.

"Did you read that at the post office?"

But I have lost him to my flower; he will not look at me or respond to anything I say. What does he make of my stomach? I wonder, back on the porch. Is he warning me, somehow, to be careful, for the baby? Don't be ridiculous, I tell myself. He read a pamphlet somewhere. He's quoting nonsense. He loves to quote—from bus schedules and instruction booklets and warranties. But then I look down and catch him staring at me, at my swollen middle beneath its green jumper. It is the first time he seems to have taken any notice, after all these months. He steps closer, jaw jutting toward me, and I call to him.

"It's a baby in there, Daniel," I say, patting my stomach. "Pretty soon it'll be out, and you can come over and see it, okay?"

"Yes," he says from the bottom step.

"You were a baby inside your mother like that."

"Yes."

Katherine told me once that he was a stranger to her—her son and yet a stranger. A stranger, and yet one she loved more than anyone else in the world. She said it the way she would say it was snowing out, as a fact blanketing her house, her world. That he was an accident, not planned, she told me swiftly on another day. For years the doctors made her think that by her thoughts she had created him unwhole. Later they took it back, said it was a neurological malfunctioning in Daniel's brain. By then the blame was deep within her bones. As a young woman she had wanted to go back to school in art history. Instead, she has given him her life. I don't know that I could be so good, so generous. Sometimes (and he's not even my son, or perhaps it's *because* he's not my son that I can think such thoughts. Does motherhood purify, rectify? I have my doubts), sometimes I want to take him by the shoulders and shake him hard until his teeth chatter and his breath comes short, just to bring a gleam of recognition to his eyes.

I need to think good thoughts, eat good food, not move more than is necessary. I need to think good thoughts.

How superstitious I've become, here on my porch, as if by keeping the channels in my head as unmuddied as clear water, my body and its guest will run a perfect course. The first time, two years ago, I wasn't like this. I went to work each day, sat before the screen, came home. Friday nights I drank a glass or two of wine.

Then I lost it in a sudden cramping, a sudden gush of blood. Afterwards I searched my blank insides for something to hold onto while Thomas cried. Now I cry at odd, hidden moments and usually only for a few seconds. Like a sneeze or a cough, it passes, sinks back down. Whether I am crying for the one I lost, or the one I might lose, or my own bad thoughts, or Daniel who is a stranger to his mother, I hardly know.

And now it is three days away from the day Thomas has marked with an exclamation point on the calendar, and I am desperate for conversation. I call up the paper to pester my friends at work, but they get other calls as soon as we start to speak. Thomas comes home for lunch, and I almost ask him to stay longer, but my pride won't let the words escape my mouth. I make myself some tea. I leave messages on my mother's and my sister Jen's machines.

And then it is three-fifteen, and I see Daniel standing in the yard, leaning his head in my direction again, looking at my stomach. I am proud, in the oddest, most illogical way, to have entered his consciousness and become more interesting than the flowers that I plant. I am a physical phe-

nomenon, suddenly, more than just myself. He comes up
the porch steps and stands by the wall of the house. He
hands me a magazine.

"Thank you, Daniel." It is *Time,* an issue he has already
brought. I put it down.

"You're welcome, Carlotta."

"Is your mother home yet? I didn't see her car."

145

He leans toward the wall. "My mother has a doctor's
appointment and will be home at four-thirty or four forty-
five."

"Oh. Do you have your key?"

But once more I have lost him, his concentration taken
by something else. He clenches and unclenches his fists
and tilts his body toward the wall. I look, but see nothing
there, just the peeling white clapboard of the house. Then I
listen—for it seems to be his ear and not his eye that seeks
the wall—and detect a faint chirping sound. The crickets
are everywhere this summer, waking me each morning
with their scraping wings.

"That's a cricket in the wall, Daniel," I say. "Do you like
that noise?"

But he doesn't hear me. He has begun to imitate the
insect to himself, echoing its sound in a deft chirp-chirping
of his throat.

I sit in my chair and listen to this duet playing back and
forth between the invisible cricket and Daniel—a counter-
point so steady, so rhythmic, it's hard to tell which sound
comes from outside the wall, which sound from within. I
don't know how long it goes on; it lulls me—perhaps I'll
fall asleep. I shut my eyes. This is, I hope, what the early
part of labor will be like, hours suspended, breath the only
clock, in and out with such steadiness, such regularity, that
progress becomes a sort of by-product. You simply breathe.
Then things move faster (I've seen films, read books, imagined. I have no idea, really, what it will be like). Breath
grows jagged, back is arched, fingers clenched to palms.
Give in, they tell us at my childbirth class. *To the rhythm,*

to your body. Let yourself go. But where exactly, I wonder, do you go when you let yourself, and how do you get back?

I am knocked from my thoughts by his head beating hard against the wall.

He is thumping the back of his head against the place where the noise came out—not gently, not to make a point, but hard, his neck snapping back with force, his skull banging over and over against the flaking paint of the white house. His palms, too, bang flat against the wall. He lets out a stream of high-pitched chirping sounds.

Get up, I tell myself. Calm him, get him to stop. I hold onto the sides of the chair and lift myself. A pain darts through my middle, between my legs. Jesus, I think, don't let my water break. I walk toward him, put a hand on his shoulder to steady him.

"Stop it, Daniel! You'll hurt yourself!" I hear my shrill voice saying, and then he has shoved me back, and I am falling, groping for balance, feeling for the wall, for the edge of the chair. My fingers close around its wicker back.

And he is hitting the wall with the back of his head again, each thump punctuated by a shrieking sound, his hands flapping loose before my face. I lean over myself, over my baby. His noise is piercing us; his hands could capsize us, could knock us flat. I want to bare my teeth and growl. I would bind his wrists, kick him in the groin if I thought I could lift my leg that high—anything to get him to go home.

Instead I lurch forward and slap him hard against the cheek.

On his face, the purest confusion, a terrible bewilderment. As if he'd never seen a hand before, never seen a woman or a porch. As if my hand had dropped like a hard, pale chip of planet from the sky.

I inch my way across the porch and behind the wall, inside my house, behind the screen door. I lock the screen door, lock the other door behind it. As I watch through the window in the door, he pushes aside the chair, turns toward the wall again and leans his forehead up against the paint.

He sobs—not the kind of sobs I know, wrenched from some human center, some site of connection and disconnection—but the tearless sobs of a man whose sorrow comes from behind walls, through radio dials and objects moved by a careless hand. Dry sobs, rhythmic as his chirps or the beating of his head against the house. If I didn't equate crying with pain, I would think these sobs were almost comforting, the way the steady movement of a night train or rocking chair brings sleep with continual motion. I lean my back against the inside of the door and listen to him cry. My own tears, when they come, are the opposite of Daniel's: silent, wet, my body turning inside out. I cannot hear myself, but I taste the salty liquid with my tongue.

When I look out on the porch again, Daniel is gone. Soon I hear Katherine's car pull into the drive. She comes over before dinner and asks me what happened.

"Listen, I'm really sorry," she says when I tell her about the cricket and headbanging. "He's been fine lately, but I still shouldn't have left him on his own."

How did she know to come to me? Did Daniel talk to her? Did a watchful neighbor give her a report? I haven't told her that I slapped him, but when I picture Daniel I see an imprint of my hand upon his face.

"What happened?" I ask her. "Why did he get so upset?"

"I don't know," she says. "I guess it's either because of extreme pleasure or extreme pain, or some very fine line between the two. You know—like his music."

I must look puzzled, because she says she thought she had told me and explains how Daniel, in listening to the radio, has devised a system of rooms and doors. If there are spoken voices on the broadcast, he can listen in the same room as the machine. For classical music, he must go one room away and shut the door. Pop music demands two or three rooms, depending on the song. For the Beatles, Daniel shuts four doors. In the middle of winter his parents find him quivering with cold and joy on the front porch, his ear cocked to a quatri-filtered "Lucy in the Sky with Diamonds." Asked to come inside, he will clench his teeth together and press his fists against his mouth.

"The Beatles?" I say. "Are they even played much anymore?"

Katherine smiles. "No, thank God. If they were on all the time, our family would crack."

I tell her about the cricket, and she says yes, Daniel has a thing about crickets, the way he has a thing about the noise a sewing machine makes, the refrigerator's whir, the thud of a newspaper being tossed onto a porch.

"Why?" I ask. "Do you have any idea?"

She shrugs, a quick shrug, almost coy, so that I get a glimpse of what she must have been like as a younger woman—bright and playful, wry. "It turns him on, I guess. He goes for some noises, and others drive him crazy, like he's oversensitized or something. He once told me his skin hurt when he was touched."

"I guess maybe it stopped chirping. He might have gotten so upset because it stopped."

"Maybe. Or maybe it kept chirping, and he liked it so much he couldn't stand it. Or else you interrupted him, and his frustration was too much. It's hard to tell."

"Listen, I've got to tell you something."

"It's okay," she says.

"No, it's not. I—I slapped him. I just completely panicked—"

"Yeah, I know. He told me."

"He told you? How did he—I mean what exactly did he say?"

"I found him curled in his room under a quilt, and I coaxed him into telling me what happened, and he said he went to work and sorted through nine-hundred-and-thirty-two letters and ate his sandwich and came home and found a cricket and was slapped by Carlotta."

"Was he angry?"

"Oh come on, Carlotta."

"I know, but I mean, how did he say it?"

"He recounted it."

"Yes, but he was obviously upset."

"I think it was the cricket, like you said."

"Are *you* angry?"

She shakes her head. "Just scared, I guess, but that's nothing new. It's the same old story—you know, what if something happens to us? I used to hope eventually he'd be ready to live on his own. Now I try not to think about it."

"Have you—I mean, did you ever hit him?"

She shakes her head.

"But have you ever wanted to?"

Katherine smiles. "Just about every day, and his brother too, when he was little. It doesn't mean you're an ogre. I still have to tell myself that—isn't it sad? Just wait, you'll see."

In bed that night I lie with my back against Thomas, my stomach protruding toward the cradle by the door. I can't stop shifting, and though my limbs are slack with fatigue, I know it will be hours before I sleep.

"I wish it were over," I tell him.

He says, "Me too," and I realize how hard I must be to live with sometimes, how tired he must get.

"It'll be fine," he whispers, rubbing lotion on my back. "You know how many people have done this before you? This is the least original thing you've ever done."

"Thanks."

His hands on my back are slick with lotion, smooth and flat. He coats me with moisture, then bends his hands and climbs his fingers up my vertebrae. All day I've ached for the safeness of this touching, this seeking not of openings but of smooth expanses, the desert stretches of my skin. A few doors away, Daniel, whose skin hurts when you touch him, is probably asleep. What dreams can such a one dream—full of noises and puffed blossoms, white letters stacked in piles, numbered boxes waiting to be filled? And the one inside me, can it be dreaming too, and if so, where does its pleasure lie, and what does it do to stave the pleasure off, when pleasure becomes more than it can stand?

I go from bed to porch, from porch to bed, until finally it is the morning of the exclamation point on the calendar, but nothing will happen today, I can tell. I rise, make my tea, go out to the front porch. I did not go out there yesterday or the day before, but sat on the back screened porch where I would not see anyone, where I would not be seen. Thomas wanted to stay home today to drive me to the hospital, but I told him not to be silly—nothing ever happens when it's supposed to, and I can always call. Now I go out to my chair on the front porch. I listen but hear no cricket, only a car honking in the distance and the rustling of trees in the slight, moist wind. Daniel stands watch over my flower, lunch bag and umbrella on the grass by his feet. Perhaps I should be afraid of him now, but he is too familiar; even in his rage he was too familiar, like something I'd been in another life. I wonder if he has already forgotten about the cricket and my slap. Perhaps he remembers and has grown afraid of me.

"Hello, Daniel," I say.

"Hello, Carlotta."

"Today I'm supposed to have my baby."

He leans down over the flower. Why this flower, I wonder again. Why my garden, and not the garden on the other side?

"Did you hear me, Daniel? Today I'm supposed to have my baby."

"Yes."

"What do you think—do you think I'll have it today?"

"Yes." He straightens up and looks at his watch.

"You don't want to be late," I tell him. "Bye."

"Good-bye, Carlotta."

"I'll see you at three-fifteen when you get home, okay?"

"Yes."

MUSIC FOR FOUR DOORS

I'll see him at three-fifteen, or perhaps I will not see him—maybe the mark on the calendar is right, and I won't be home. One of these days, today or tomorrow or the next, my life will change so that I'll hardly recognize it, hardly recognize myself. Still, in the mornings until the first frost, Daniel will stare down at my platycodon. I am grateful for this knowledge, would thank him if I thought he could fathom what I meant.

Now he is threading his wrist through the loop handle of his yellow umbrella, scanning the sky, kneeling to roll the top of his paper lunch bag in a tight, neat coil. Then he is large on the sidewalk, steady as he goes—and has rounded the corner out of sight.

THE COUNTING GAME

I can feel I will be called on before it happens from a sort of bunching in the air, a pressure, like fabric caught in a broken sewing machine, puckering in on itself. Then all the necks swivel, all the hair swings round, and if I am in France my answer comes to me in English, and if I am in England or South Africa my answer comes to me in French. On the floor where I stare down, I see ink cartridges, paper clips, buttons—things nobody cares enough to pick up, but not exactly rubbish either. I narrow the world to these objects—their metal or plastic bodies, their slight weights. Sometimes I whisper "I don't know." Sometimes all I can muster is a shrug.

It happened in England at Dollis Junior School, where the wool of the green school uniform gave me a pink rash; it happened in Johannesburg where there were only twelve of us left after a while, my brother and I stuck in the same form, and he much quicker on his feet. Here at the lycée on the outskirts of Paris in Neuilly-sur-Seine it has happened eight times so far. The teacher massages his temples and stares at the ceiling; this will not do, such self-indulgent behavior, such new-girl antics—the first time, maybe, was understandable, but the second time was really quite enough. "She should know better," I can feel the teacher thinking, "at seventeen."

What they don't know is that I *do* talk, scream even, "Get out! *Vas-t'en!*" to my brother Jean in my highest pitch until he covers his ears, makes his police siren noise, and rushes from my room. In my sleep, I am told, I let entire sentences escape, whole conversations, sometimes in English, sometimes in French. My sister comes to my bed and shakes me by the shoulder, and I wake confused, wondering what I've said.

They say: If you want to function in this society, if you want to pass your bac, you must work very hard in school and conquer this timidity of yours. Too much, they say, *tu exagères*, and they sigh the way my grandmother does when we don't finish our fish or cabbage.

Ma chérie, ma biche, mon chou-chou. For a long time I thought it was my mother's private language of affection, to be spoken behind closed doors in our houses in England or South Africa. If you can't fall asleep, said my mother, think of nonsense words, and I thought of *vent frais, vent du matin, vent qui souffle en haut des grands pins.* Fresh wind, morning wind up in the pines. Somewhere I knew what it meant, but sound covered meaning and sleep came.

"What do you think *in!*" asked my cousin Claudine after we had come "home" two months ago, and I said I didn't know, but this wasn't altogether true.

When I think of or speak to my mother and my brother, it is usually in French. I was born in Paris, so was Jean. I use English when I think of my father, from Devon, and my little sister Sophie, who was born in London and has lived in South Africa for four of her six years. I am simplifying; really, it is more of a blur. My own thoughts, my conversations with myself, are even more difficult to track. Lately, when I am making an effort, I think in French. When I am homesick, sick of having no home to be sick for, my thoughts come in English—the language with the hardest edges, but also the saddest language, the one people everywhere speak in mangled snatches, the language of visa restrictions and emergency procedures, of airports and custom lines.

In Johannesburg we had a white house with a swimming pool, seven bedrooms, and two maids. When my mother was out I brought the maids my tape recorder, and they laughed in the kitchen, two Zulu women, and asked me to play back their laughs. Afternoons, there were shark shows I was not allowed to see, but Jean and I went anyway when we were supposed to be at activities hour at the church. First they showed the grainy, flickering film of the sharks nosing through the water and banging against the metal bars of the cameraman's cage. Then the curtain was pulled aside to reveal the real shark corpse spread out on a long, white table, and they began to cut open its stomach and hold things up: a shoe, five coins, a human femur bone. It was there every time, that same bloodied bone, jammed down the shark's throat just before the show, probably, but still the tourists always gasped, and Jean and I, knowing it was coming, always gasped as well.

In some countries I look exotic, and in others, like England, I look average, but here in France I just look wrong. The French girls have swingy hair and wide, clear foreheads. They wear starched ironed jeans with ballet flats, padded velvet headbands, and clean sweatshirts covered with slogans in English. I have frizzy hair—too blond, so blond it's almost white—and a long, sort of pinched-up face. I blush when I sneeze too loud, when I walk down the hall, when I take my tray from the lunch line to a table, weaving through all those elbows and hands.

My father sits me down in my grandmother's kitchen and says, "You must talk in school, Alice. If you don't talk, you won't pass your baccalaureate. If you don't pass, you'll never go to university. That's how it works here, understand? You'll end up limited for life."

What he is really saying is For Christ's sake, we've moved back here for your sake, to give you stability, a place to go to university. If you were as smart as your brother, as adaptable as your sister . . . He has taken a pay cut from his bank, given things up for this. There is even talk of buying a house.

I want to ask *where* I will be limited for life, why this should be the place above all others, how I am to go about

156

the vague task of making myself at home. I picture Finland, where other people are as pale and blond as I am, and the snow muffles sound. Or Alaska, where there is a greater variety of wildlife than anywhere else on earth. I know things about Alaska—the pipeline, the Eskimos, the pack dogs, the igloos, the many ways to say snow. I once read a book on it. But when they asked me at lycée, it was as if someone had taken a block of ice, taken the whole frozen tundra, and jammed it down my throat. "*Je ne sais pas,*" I answered, my mind an enormous chilly blank.

Once, in South Africa, I found the maid crouched in the bathroom pulling bits of my yellow hair from the tub drain to put in a handkerchief in her net bag. She said it was to show her children, to put on their rag dolls, but at night I imagined her doing spells with my hair, against me, back in one of those tiny red or blue houses in Soweto where the blacks are made to live. I drove through once with Father John to hand out toys—each house the size of my own room. In Neuilly they think I must be racist because of where I've lived, but I don't think I am, only afraid of being hated. There, the maids hated me quietly, behind my back, in languages I couldn't understand. Here, where my sin is that I have arrived too late and said too little, the students hate me face on, with open eyes.

"You're inventing," my mother says when I complain. "How can they hate you? They don't even know you."

And I think: Hasn't she learned anything anywhere?

In Johannesburg we gave the maids our outgrown clothes and shoes for their children, and they held them up, sniffed them, and tossed away the worn or musty ones—no thank you, missy— threw them in the basket meant for rags. During the water shortage Jean, Sophie, and I snuck out when it was dark to throw illegal buckets of water on the grass. "Watch for the Grobbelaar's dogs," our father cautioned, but Anna, the younger maid, had told Sophie that the dogs would only go for the blacks, and it was so silent out there, not a growl, not a bark. We children didn't see the point, for the grass was dead and there was not enough water, but at least we got to go outside for ten minutes in our fenced-in garden.

"We can't let it all just shrivel up and die," our mother said, and nobody pointed out that it was already too late.

It was not, our parents thought, a place for children to grow up. So many whites—the bankers, the diplomats— were moving back to where they'd come from; each month our little private school got smaller, the forms merging until we all had brothers and sisters looking over our shoulders. Each day at five o'clock the Moslems kneeled on their sidewalk rugs as the loudspeaker prayer truck came round, and the office workers took the sound as a cue and went out to get their coffee. It was a Thursday, my father starting back with a cup in hand, when the top floor of his building was bombed, nine people killed. Half a block away, the noise startled my father into spilling coffee on his arm. At dinner he rolled up his sleeve to show us the red splotch below his elbow. The company said they would switch us to Australia or Canada, but my father said no.

"We need to give them a bit of stability," he told headquarters over the phone, and I thought of Ile de Ré, the island off France where we had stayed at my grandmother's summer house for three weeks out of every summer of my life—my fixed point, my point of reference, all I knew of this country where I was born. Later, when I knew we were moving, I still pictured Neuilly like Ile de Ré, though I knew it would be different, imagined bicycles spotted with sea salt, old whitewashed houses with green shutters lining the lanes as if they had formed there out of nature, erupted like the island from the sea.

To start with, we are staying in my grandmother's winter home, a large flat in a six-story gray stone building with a tiny mirrored lift. The sea is hours away in any direction, though the Bois de Boulogne is nearby with its artificial lakes. After dinner my parents keep us in, conditioned by the thought of danger lurking close at hand. For daytime

157

use they bought me an orange métro pass with my photo stapled to it, but I walk when I can. The métro frightens me—the smell of urine, the one-way doors, bands playing loud in the corridors, all those people pressing close.

My parents find a tutor for me, a university student studying English. She will quiz me on math, literature, and history if I will speak to her in English and correct her mistakes. They are paying her something as well. The point is, she will get me to talk. She tells me in English that her boyfriend is from America. Her English is not bad. She looks nothing like the girls in my class, her hair long and curly, her nose thin and pointed like an elf's. She wears noisy earrings, clusters of tiny silver bells, and my mother looks at her skeptically when she first comes through the door, but she has been recommended by a friend of my grandmother's who says she is from a good family and bright. Her name is Natalie. We sit in the guest bedroom I share with my sister, and she asks me what my interests are. I mumble, in English, "I don't know."

"I mean, what sort of things do you like?" she asks in French, and I say guitar and tennis, neither of which is true, but they sound right, and then I add reading, which is true but sounds so boring.

"Tell me about South Africa," she says, and when I ask what she wants to know, she says, "Well, is it as bad as they say?"

"I guess so," I answer, shrugging, wondering exactly what they say. "I guess we left because it was pretty bad."

We begin with math and go on to history. She leans forward and stares into my eyes as she speaks. In school I have worked hard at math and done all right, especially in geometry, where I like the shapes—vectors moving off into infinity; neat, symmetrical triangles; how an angle pulled apart until it's lying flat becomes a line. I answer most of her questions correctly. History, though, is such a blur to me, so much to keep track of, too many countries, so many events come and gone. Natalie seems to know every king, every queen and duke of France. My mother has appeared in the doorway. Sophie is leaning at her side.

"She has some catching up to do, no?" asks my mother, and Natalie nods.

"It's been hard for her," says my mother. "We've moved so much, and this one always has her head in the clouds. Each time, at her new school, she takes the diagnostic test, and they place her above average, and then she finds she's behind the others in this or that." She sighs. "With a little concentration she'll catch right up. I keep telling her, eh Alice?"

She she she, I chant silently to myself. *Elle elle elle elle elle.*

"She can't talk," announces Sophie. "She gets sick," and I scream at her inside my head, push her round body up against the doorway. Later I will get her for real.

"Timid." Natalie states it as if it were the name of a well-known town.

"Speak English to her now, chérie," says my mother. "Tell her about your old school."

Summoned and exhibited like this, I lose my voice, and I push past them, stand in the hall, and stare down at the doorway at the end. I feel something on my shoulder, Natalie's hand.

"It doesn't matter," she says. She tugs gently on my hair and leaves.

Each Wednesday afternoon, when I have half days at school, Natalie comes out from Paris. She never actually says she hates being in my grandmother's flat with its enormous wooden armoires, musty beds, and heavy drapes. Instead, she says she needs to smoke; can we go to a café, or isn't it lovely out; shall we go for a stroll around the Bois de Boulogne? They are posed as questions, but she never waits for me to answer. My mother worries briefly, then decides it is all right as long as we stay in the neighborhood. One day Natalie says she has something to show me. "Come," she tells me. "It'll be so fast," so we take the métro to her room in a student boardinghouse in the city, and she shows me charcoal sketches and asks may she draw my face? She recounts stories about her friends and throws in school questions now and then, mostly math, which she knows I can handle. I do not need to talk, hardly at all, except quick answers to her math questions and translations for her language questions, the words you never learn in school: *degueuler, foutre*—puke and screw. Her boyfriend has already taught her most of it, but I can tell she likes to make me say the words and watch me blush.

"Don't be a puritan, Alice," she tells me in English. "How old are you now, eh? Oh, here is one he told to me: *loosen up.*"

She draws me, but crumples up the paper before I have a chance to see. "No good," she says. "We'll try again next time."

At school the teachers stop calling on me out of kindness, boredom, or frustration. A few times I do better than usual on an exam, and they praise me out loud, but then they stop that, too, since I bite my lip and cover my cheek with my hand. Stop, I tell myself. Stop it. It is not that I think I am worse than the others. They know so little about anything. Most of the students are white; a few are Arab, Indian, or black. We live in a fancy neighborhood, so the nonwhites are either the rich children of diplomats and bankers or the poor children of concierges. One boy in my class swears he is a prince, and I believe him from the way he holds his head. The woman who mops the corridors is from Martinique and has four children who go to the school. I dawdle by her in the hall as she pushes her broom; she is the most familiar face around. She has a flowered apron tied around her tiny waist, a crocheted brown hat pushed down over her forehead. She says she is tired all the time, something wrong with her legs.

"You're a new one, where have you come from?" she asks, her accent lilting, and when I tell her South Africa, she peers at my face as if to discover something there, then looks disappointed, for I reveal nothing, do not know what to reveal. She plants one hand on her hip and pushes her broom away.

I must begin to think in French, but I find it so difficult. Not that the words aren't there, but they aren't friendly and to use them says too much: time to settle down, time to talk, time to live inside a country as if it were a skin. Sophie comes home with friends named Marie-Laure and Victoire. They play clapping games with complex rhyming songs in the courtyard. Jean plays rugby in the Bois.

Natalie invites me to a film and to spend the night in the fourteenth arrondissement in her student boarding house. When my grandmother and my parents say no, I leave the table, go to my room to pout. My father comes in.

"We worry about you, love, that's all," he says. I am silent. He leans down and scoops up one of the cats.

"It's a big city," he tells me. "You don't know the customs. Natalie and her friends are older."

I flip through the pages of a book and watch the print blur. "How do you expect me to do anything?" I ask.

He ponders this, places the cat on his shoulder. "Yes, I know, which is why I've decided you may go with her, but not to any old trashy film. We'll get a *Pariscope* and find you something good."

I smile inwardly, nod solemnly to my father; all along I knew I would win, only a question of details and time. I close the book, shoo the cat out, and follow my father back to dinner. Sophie claps at the victory, but already I am beginning to panic. Will Natalie come fetch me? Will I have to take the métro into the city at night? Will all her friends be there, her boyfriend whose sketch I've seen? I have imitated the girls at school and begun to wear sweatshirts covered with sailboats and advertisements for American health clubs and ski resorts. This is clearly inappropriate; Natalie wears black jeans, blouses with gauzy sleeves like wings, antique lace nighties as shirts, men's suit jackets with the collar up.

On Friday night I sneak into my brother's room and take out a tweed jacket and a white T-shirt. I tie my hair back with a scarf the way Natalie has suggested, to get it off my face. I am quite exotic, really, with my hair this way, my hands in my pockets, my shoulders hunched up a little, a quiet smile on my lips. I roll up the cuffs of the jacket to show the silky lining, black and iridescent as a crow's wing. I pull strands of hair down around my face, sort of pale and mysterious, slightly undone. Somebody could make a certain kind of film star out of me. Or perhaps I look ridiculous; I'm not sure. The hair should look messy, but not too.

Natalie fetches me. We do not go to a film, though we stand outside the cinema and read the poster and review so I can report back to my parents. We sit in a café on Boulevard Raspail and drink *cassis* and beer. There are so many of us, of them, twenty people perhaps, and they are all talking at once, about cinema, a student strike, a new advertisement by Chanel, Babette's baby, the job Antoine got at the FNAC. I don't follow much of it, but nobody seems to notice me except Natalie, who keeps her hand on my knee, and her boyfriend Andy, who can't handle such a rush of French and asks me polite questions in English: How long have I been here? Natalie tells him I'm studying for my bac; do I know what I'll do when I get out?

He is almost as blond as I am, almost as pale, and slightly shorter than Natalie, with a tiny gold hoop hanging from his ear. His grin is crooked and sweet. He is not frightening, not at all, and yet he frightens me. Not handsome, not in a typical way, yet though I would not have pictured him like this (her sketch told me nothing), I see he is perfect for her, as perfect as she is. Her other hand is on his knee, toying with the frayed part of his jeans, working its way through the tangle of white thread to the skin. To them I look as if I am concentrating on their faces, but in fact I see other things as well—feet touching feet, the way people lean, a column of ash growing long on a cigarette.

THE COUNTING GAME

At eleven they all toss money into the center of the table to pay the bill, then rise, and I follow. They turn up the street, and when I look at Natalie she smiles and pulls me by the sleeve. Outside the café there was a lot of bustle, but now we walk past rows of quiet buildings like the ones in Neuilly, a few closed shops, a school. We come to a square—I have been there before. Two enormous stone lions flank the intersection; there is a glowing métro sign: Denfert-Rochereau. We stand in a group on the sidewalk. They stop. One of them runs across and disappears down a stairway. Two minutes later someone whistles. Natalie grabs my arm again and whispers, "Run!"

Then we are crossing the street, descending a spiral staircase into blackness, going through an open door where the air turns slightly sour, damp, into a darkness so thick that I let out a small gasp and grab for Natalie's hand, which closes around mine and squeezes my fingers. "Natalie?" I whisper.

"Andy," says the hand's owner. "It's okay. We're in now. She went on ahead."

Natalie's voice comes to me from the other side. "This, Alice," she calls, saying my name as if it were all created for me, "this is the Catacombs, where they store the Paris dead." She speaks like a tour guide, knowing and instructive, in her tutor mode. This is where, she tells me, when the charnel houses got too full in 1785, they moved the bones and organized them into halls; then, during the war, La Résistance had its headquarters here. Now, by day, there are tourist tours. By night, well, Étienne has a friend who has a friend who is a cop who made a wax cast of the key.

Someone turns on a flashlight, and I look around. It is almost like being in an underwater cave, like the films of the African sharks. The walls are brown and damp, rounded like uneven rock, but then I look more closely and see that the rounded parts are the tops of skulls, the knobby parts the ends of femur bones, the whole thing carefully patterned: femur, femur, femur, skull, femur, like a mosaic in a church. We all walk together down a hall. Here and there are posted bronze plaques: Diderot, Sartre, Pascal on death.

I know I am supposed to feel a horror, a shiver, a dark chill, but instead I feel little but the nicest feeling of belonging—how they have let me come with them, how Andy has not let go of my hand. When it gets too narrow he falls behind me but keeps one hand on the small of my back. Natalie leads, up front. They begin to sing:

> *C'est une maison bleue*
> *Adossée à la colline,*
> *On y vient à pied,*
> *On ne frappe pas,*
> *Ceux qui vivent là*
> *Ont jeté la clé . . .*

Andy says he doesn't get it, and I translate—a blue house crouched on a hill, we arrive on foot, we don't knock, they've thrown out the key. I, too, know the song from my summers on Ile de Ré, a sixties song from the days when everyone lived together with no locks. I wasn't born yet, then, but the song has stuck around. These people sing it as if they believe every word, as if they are living it. It echoes loud.

"Sing," says Andy, but I shake my head.

Then we are at a juncture, a meeting place of two tunnels, and there, in mid-song, the whole group separates, people stepping into shadows, still singing, but now the song becomes disjunctive and begins to bounce off itself.

"Hey," I say to Andy. "What's going on?"

He leads me into a hollow in the wall, big enough to stand in, but we crouch. He leans back and rubs his head against the empty heads, the bones. The thought comes to me: how this is their closest brush with horror, and they have gone to such lengths to get the key. I reach out and close my hand over the top of a skull. So smooth, so hard, like a water-worn stone or the head of a wooden African doll. It is not quite even, full of slight aberrations and bumps. I have never seen dead bodies, except in photographs; we were always kept in during the riots. I have seen dead sharks, sought them out, but the shark show was different—animal, predator, tourist trap, all in the spirit of fun. Or at least I thought so; now I'm not so sure. Andy pulls me back against him; we both stare out into the dark.

"You okay?" he asks. I nod and (how brave I am sometimes, how outrageously forward, I hardly know myself) reach for his hand. When I grab hold of it, he strokes my fingers for a moment, then sighs and presses his mouth against the back of my neck. I dip my head back toward him.

"You're really very sweet, aren't you?" he whispers.

I shrug, and he kisses my neck again. "You know I've never met anyone like Natalie before," he says.

I try to say I know, neither have I. Instead I say, "*Ça ne fait rien*"—it doesn't matter—but my words are covered by the slow beginnings of accumulated sound.

They are calling numbers. It takes me a few minutes to figure out the pattern: First one voice shouts "*un,*" and another calls "*sept,*" then a third adds the two numbers and calls out "*huit,*" the sum. A fourth voice calls a random number, and a fifth voice adds that number to the last sum. Then a sixth voice calls a random number, and a seventh adds, on and on.

The voices seem to be speaking in order down the tunnels, like dominoes collapsing in a row. Andy is still holding me, more loosely now, and we crouch and listen as if to bird songs or warnings telling us to stay inside. The numbers grow. I hear Natalie's voice call forty-five, then someone very near me calls out nineteen. I move away from Andy, stand in the middle of the tunnel and wait.

"*Soixante-quatre,*" calls a voice even closer, and I know it is about to be my turn.

I could call anything, any random number. For a second I think about calling something complicated with decimals or fractions, or in a language they would not understand.

Then, as I stand there, the silence grows stretched and angry, and I try instead to think of anything, the simplest number, as if I were a child trying to remember how to count.

The point is to keep things moving in sequence; it hardly even matters what you say.

Inside my head I yell: *"Trois-cent,"* but my lips are sealed shut and I can almost see the number lodged inside my mouth, the swollen zeros straining to get out. As the silence grows around me, I realize that I cannot imagine the sound—the pitch, the tone, the age—of my own voice.

"I think it's your turn," says Andy, nudging me, and I sidestep him and whisper fiercely that he should go.

"Shit," he says. "I haven't been following."

"Any number," I whisper. *"Un, deux,* Go—"

And for Andy, a foreigner, a tattered traveler not expected to belong, it is easy—a bright *"quatre"* in his American accent. It echoes, his voice steady, strong, and clear, and the stalled game lurches into motion again, moving away from us down the hall. The numbers keep mounting, higher and higher. Andy and I crouch again, not touching, side by side.

"When it reaches exactly one thousand," he says, "they'll call it quits."

"Mille," I tell him, and he says he knows.

Later I go with them to Natalie's room in the student boardinghouse; I will sleep alone there while she sleeps at Andy's several blocks away. When they drop me off, they look at me like worried parents and ask me if I'm all right. I am afraid they have taken an interest in me as something to develop, a kind of hobby—we'll make her blossom, it'll be such fun. I should warn them that though I blink too much and look down, I am not a frightened flower. If they dig deep enough they will find much that is tart and judgmental—if only I were as sweet as I look.

I am grateful for the secretness of thought; if they knew my thoughts they might drop me forever, and I want so badly to be their friend. Even now they are about to leave.

Stay, I want to beg them. *One of you, both of you. Not because you feel you should, but because you want to.* They are people with light around them, people I'd like to be. I blush when each of them kisses me, tell them thanks. They look at each other and smile. *I'm sorry,* I think to Natalie. *I took his hand.* I picture Andy's torso beneath my fingers, his pale skin. Natalie gives me a hug, and I can feel her jealousy in her shoulder blades, as no doubt she can feel mine.

"You'll come out with us again," she says, and I nod. They leave and walk along the street, mount the stairs to his room, climb into bed, and lie there on top of each other, locked in each other's arms. I can see it all. If they stop to talk, it will be to compare notes on the evening.

I want to hear. And I'm afraid and do not want to hear.

It is not the first time this has happened to me, this making of friends, this settling in. It happened in Johannesburg with an American girl, Lynne, whose father was a journalist. For five months we told each other secrets, then she left. It happened, too, with Avtar, the Indian boy who tended our garden there last summer. With him I didn't have to talk, but we touched each other's feet behind the tool shed—his smooth, long, and brown, mine white with blue veins, and he ran his fingers along my arches until my spine ached, then trailed his hand on my leg, up under my skirt until half his arm was hidden from view. Neither of us said a word, but for days he came back until the garden was pruned and empty in the drought, nothing left to do. It would surprise my parents, all this, surprise my teachers, who do not know what to make of me at all. I am not playing games, exactly, because I cannot help it.

Sitting around waiting for things to play themselves out is what I do not know how to do. I am more like my mother, who prides herself on her mastery of the art of packing, the whole household boxed and labeled in a day. Now I am supposed to settle in. Natalie's boardinghouse is quiet, not a sound from the hall or the rooms of the girls next door, everyone still out or already asleep. I will not stay in this country for long. I will find a country with a brand-new language and an alphabet I cannot make any sense of, with lettering like Arabic or Chinese. Then I will learn from textbooks and imitation, the first sounds like the ones a child makes, then simple sentences, phrases strung together, a whole paragraph, numbers up to one million and beyond. First I will fail my bac and leave the exam room without a word. Then I will pick my country and go there, and because I have chosen it, it will be mine from the beginning, and I will attract friends like steel shavings to a magnet and never leave. Enough gestures accumulated eventually become something like habits apart from thought. I have never stayed long enough to see it happen, but I am sure it does.

I am so lucky, only seventeen, and I've seen so much. This is what Natalie tells me, but she also feels sorry for me, gives me advice on how to dress and do my hair.

"Pretend I'm the teacher," she said the other week during our lesson in a café, and she put on a stern face and waved a pen at me. "Discuss attitudes toward realism in Balzac and Flaubert."

I shook my head. "Can I have a cigarette?"

She thinks she has started me smoking, something she is proud of since it represents my loosening up. I have not told her that I did it in South Africa with my brother and the maids.

"Realism," said Natalie. "*Vas-y.*"

And I could tell she was frustrated, didn't understand me, where my limits were, why I couldn't just take a deep breath and go. If change were an easy thing, it would have happened everywhere. Natalie was born in this city, has been here all her life. Andy will have to stay in France to be with her, in Paris; she cannot imagine living anywhere else.

Across from her in the café that day, I thought about Flaubert. I remembered some things—so much hatred in that man, how he wanted to pour boiling water into the throats of the bourgeoisie.

"Here's a hint," she told me, opening her notebook. "He said 'reality, if we are to reproduce it well, must enter us until we almost scream.'"

Sure, I thought. Almost. I rolled my eyes and blew an impressive series of smoke rings. Natalie squinted, watching them hover and disappear.

169

"You know you're only hurting yourself if you fail this stupid exam," she said, and I nodded. Who else would I be hurting, but I will take my hurt self in a neat bundle and transplant it. This I can carry with me, this head of mine, and it never stops talking to me, quietly, slyly, like the maids when they thought they were alone. Our house in Johannesburg is up for sale, but no one wants to buy it, not a happy neighborhood, not a place to settle with the kids. I picture the empty swimming pool, how the blue bottom must be covered with leaves by now, half covered, all covered. How the lizards dart there; it is all they know of home. Perhaps I will go to Ile de Ré and talk to the woman who owns the fish shop, the one who has never been off the island, and now they are building a bridge to the mainland and La Rochelle.

"What do I need a bridge for?" she said to my mother last summer as she folded paper around a slab of fish.

Like a barnacle I will attach myself to the side of the woman's shop, or no, to the side of her husband's boat. That way I will move through the ocean, days, but always come back at night. So much of the world is allowed to be silent—the barnacle, the boat, the fish, the flickering celluloid sharks. So much of the world is dead, and it is silent too—the brown skulls, the knobby femur bones. Femur, femur, femur, skull, femur. It is only a way to organize, nothing romantic, nothing horrific, only a game. It is like adding numbers up, a way to put things together and go on.

I count out loud in Natalie's room in my two languages,

weaving numbers: "un, two, trois," then add some Afri-
kaans I learned from our neighbors in Johannesburg and
keep on alternating: "vier, vyf, six, seven, huit . . . " I will
not mess up, not loosen up, not scream. I will count. Such a
strong voice I have when I make a little effort, almost a
deep voice, like that of an orator or an actress, or someone
who needs quite badly to be heard. No one can hear me,
except maybe the girl in the room on one side of me, or the
girl in the room on the other, and though I do not mean to,
exactly, perhaps I am keeping them awake.